I'VE BROKEN ALL MY RULES FOR HER.

make you mine

ELENA M. REYES

xoxo

make you mine

SUMMARY

I should have said no:

When they asked me to take over this case and protect her with my life.
When at the sight of her, my heart beat like a war drum inside my chest.
When those light blue eyes met mine and the world stopped.
I *should've*—but I *didn't*.
And now it's too late because I've broken the rules and tasted the forbidden fruit.

I'll never let her go.

Make You Mine written by Elena M. Reyes
Original Title: Keeping Ava by Elena M. Reyes

Original Cover design by: C.M. Steele
New Cover: E.M.R.
Editor: Marti Lynch

Genre: Dark Romance/Suspense

Original Publication Date: September 2019
New Publication Date: March 24th, 2025

This is for the girlies who love an OTT protective man in a uniform. Enjoy the view, ladies. Just know many of us are jealous...

Elena XoXo

make
you
mine

TRIGGER WARNINGS:

This book contains dark subject matter that some readers might find triggering. Please read at your discretion.

Contains The Following:

FMC Witnesses A Gruesome Crime
She Is Attacked and Assaulted: One instance happens when she's 16 and the other as an adult, while she isn't raped, she is assaulted.
Forced Proximity (With MMC & She Likes It)
Explicit Violence (Some Gore)
Nightmares
Panic Attack
Serial Killer Stalking FMC
Multiple Mentions of Murdered Women
Death
Drug Use
Explicit Sex (Because I Like It Spicy)
Dark Elements and Situations
OTT Protective Detective
No Cheating

prologue

CRIME SCENE - DO NOT CROSS CRIME SCENE - DO NOT CROSS

DETECTIVE FORD

I'm restless. A little volatile.

I feel like a puppet on a string, and it has everything to do with the direct order—the witness—I've been charged with keeping safe.

Because there's just something about her...

That, and Captain Perez made his stance clear: I can't ask for a reassignment. Not that I ever would, even if I know I'm of more value to this case by hunting down the son-of-a-bitch who escaped police custody than keeping the star witness under my roof until he's caught.

For more than the obvious reasons.

Because of this need *she* evokes in me:

To protect. To avenge. To *kill* for.

The latter of which should concern me, and yet it doesn't. Just like the nervous energy currently flowing through my veins isn't because I'm annoyed with my precinct's captain. Not at all—this is the aftereffect of the file's content lying before me on the coffee table.

- **Witness: Ava Perry**
- **Age: 25**
- **From: Dallas, Texas**
- **Occupation: Owns Bakery (Cherry On Top) in a popular shopping area near her home. The location is close to where the crime was committed.**
- **Lives: Alone. Home purchased two years ago.**
- **Family: Parents deceased. Only child.**
- **Phone Number: None at the moment. Call Captain Perez if additional information is needed.**

Every line and picture—the annotations from those who compiled the information—filter through my head on an unending movie reel as I wait for my assignment to be delivered. I'm on high alert. Fucking angry. And for reasons unbeknownst to me, the horror she *witnessed* perturbs me on a personal level, no matter how hard I try to convince myself otherwise.

Not because of the victims. Not because of the nature of the case.

It's her. *Ava.*

Something about her affects me, and it's beyond my control.

I want to hunt him down and return the favor. Dismantle him limb by limb.

Closing my eyes, I exhale slowly as her face reappears behind my now-closed lids. I see how she grins at the camera, a frilly pink apron with the name *Cherry On Top* embroidered into the fabric as she stands with a large pair of scissors ready to open the door to her bakery. The sweet expression—a mirrored reflection of the simple goodness inside her—carries through every photograph inside the folder.

From her job to outings with friends and selfies, she shared on her social media accounts.

From statements taken from those who know Ava. People who are worried and care for her safety—who have first-hand knowledge of the way she curls her lip when she smiles and the dimple that immediately appears on her right cheek. Of the way her cerulean orbs always seem to shine with happiness.

So much emotion in those photographs. Each one heats the blood inside my veins for this stranger. Because I don't know this woman —have no connection to her outside this case—and yet, I feel protective of her.

The question is...

"Why?" And as of right now, I'm without a satisfying answer. There shouldn't be a single reason that goes beyond my need to serve and protect, but even those are empty platitudes. *Or maybe it's knowing just how close she came to being another name on a long list of slain females.*

A possibility, but it doesn't explain my reactions. I've never wanted to trace a finger down any woman's photograph or grin just because she does—two things I've done today and feel no shame because of it, either.

Instead, I'm eaten by the feeling that I've failed *her*, and it doesn't make a lick of sense.

It also leaves a bitter taste on my tongue.

"Son of a bitch, this is going to be a mess." Shoving the file aside, I move to stand and stretch my neck when my eyes connect with a single sheet that slid out of the folder. It has her basic information and a photograph of her driver's license, but what I'm struck by is the handwritten note at the bottom.

All women. All young. They were between the ages of nineteen

and twenty-nine with the same physical attributes: chocolate brown hair, blue eyes, and were short in stature.

A sinking feeling slams into my chest as I connect the dots to her reality:

Ava Perry is the physical embodiment of a delicate doll. Simply gorgeous.

But more than that, why he chooses each victim becomes crystal clear.

They resemble her.

She's his muse.

And I'm going to gouge out pieces of his flesh and force him to eat it.

chapter 1

AVA

Two Months Ago:
That Night...

"Jesus, it's hot," I whisper under my breath, wiping the few beads of sweat rolling down my temple. It's late and humid—quiet—and a feeling of unease fills my chest as the sudden stillness overwhelms my system.

I'm surrounded by it. Not a single, minuscule noise can be heard.

There's not so much as a stranger passing by or a car on the road, something completely at odds within the tight-knit community I call home. Because there's always someone around. Always an event or gathering, people talking while sipping coffee or having a beer, no matter what time of year it is.

Neighbors are family. End of.

Tonight, though, it feels as though the world's stopped—the beautiful town I've built my life in is empty. Desolate. Void of life.

"Wonder where everyone's tonight. Did I miss a special event announcement?" We've had those before. Have one scheduled for next weekend; the governing HOA likes to host outdoor parties or BBQ festivals at different venues near the downtown area for the families that live here.

Lifting my wrist, I check the time on my watch, and it's only fifteen minutes after seven. Not late at all, and with summer near its end, I've come to expect the scents of cooking to greet my senses the closer to home I get.

"Not tonight, I guess." Shrugging, I give my neck a quick stretch side to side before taking the next right turn. The family-oriented subdivision I'm walking through is the closest to my bakery. In a cluster of three, the communities dominate a huge roundabout with an impressive water fountain at the center—this one is the first exit, and it holds a feature none of the others do.

Beyond the charming houses adorned with quaint, seasonal outdoor decor lies a community garden I fell in love with. It's nestled between my block and the next two, toward the back end and in the middle, where there's a shortcut I take on nights like these.

My house also sits at the center of my street, and while I usually avoid low-lit areas, taking this pathway will get me there quicker than the normal route. Besides, no one hides behind a strawberry tree, much less baby ones at that. The new plants are barely visible above the ground, just leaves and a couple of vines, while tomatoes a few rows down look to be ready for picking.

Just a few more minutes, and my poor, tired body will be able to crash for the day. I need a good soak in my clawfoot—

The sudden hoot of an owl causes me to jump, its sound echoing, and I look up to find it perched atop a power line. Its presence—the way it watches me with its head slightly tilted to the side and those sharp eyes following my every move—unnerves me as I pass beneath its large body.

"Almost home," I mutter under my breath, trying to ignore the way my erratic heartbeat matches the sharp sounds the large animal emits. My hands visibly shake as I fix the strap of my cross-body bag, and yet, when a woman's scream suddenly rends the air, I freeze.

The sound is bone-chilling.

Pain-filled horror.

And fear, that unforgiving monster, takes over my limbs as everything around me goes deathly still once again. Too quiet.

What the? I cock my head, leaning back a bit to see if another sound follows, but I'm met with nothing. A deathly nothing. An eerie nothing outside of a more subdued hoot from the owl still perched above me.

"Keep walking, Ava. It's more than likely someone watching a horror flick nearby." *Maybe it's coming from the house a little farther up.* I force myself to take a step, and then another, cursing my newest shop assistant for burning two trays of orange cranberry muffins until they were nothing more than a charred crisp—an incident/disaster that's taught me two valuable lessons as I mentally repeat that I'm safe.

Cleaning trays with burned fruit is a nightmare. That, and I should've filled my gas tank instead of deciding a late evening stroll was good for me after a day of nibbling on treats because right now, as I rush through the empty garden, I feel idiotic.

Especially on a night when it seems the neighborhood is desolate.

"Keep calm. Nothing's wrong…just keep walking." It leaves me on a gasp when the heavy crash of something metal and then glass rings through the air, followed quickly by another sharp scream of pain. My eyes shift, my mind running frantically while trying to pinpoint where the danger is coming from, and that's when I notice I've taken a wrong turn.

This exit leads to two-story homes on what looks to be a cul-de-sac, and the lot beside me on the left seems under heavy remodel as I step onto the paved road. Moreover, the overgrowth partially blocks my view past what's a few feet from me. This is also out of the norm in a neighborhood where every lawn is manicured to look exactly like its neighbors.

No weeds.

No leaves.

No garbage.

My hand trembles as I pull out an old cell phone from my back pocket, and even more so when I dial 911. An operator answers, asking me how he can help, but words evade me.

It's hard to breathe, much less answer past the knot in my throat.

"Please stop!" the woman being attacked cries out, and my chest grows tight. I still can't see them.

"Shut the fuck up," a male voice growls out, and the sound of a hard smack comes seconds after. She sobs, the garbled pleas becoming louder, and I can't explain why it sounds as if they're closer. "You deserve this and so much more, whore. Now beg."

Oh God. I begin to shake because I know this voice. The low timbre conjures images of him coming into my shop. Of him asking me out on a date various times in the last few months.

The way he told me just this morning that someday I would be *his.*

The bakery's bell chimes above the entrance, signaling a new customer, and I look up, almost cringing when Jason's eyes immediately meet mine. He's a loyal customer at Cherry On Top, always too polite, yet his flirting borders on pushy. Not that he's done anything, but the vibe is always there.

Off. Weird. Creepy.

Or maybe it's all me.

Either way, I'm always wary, and the smile on my face is fake yet professionally acceptable. "Morning, Mr. Ripley. What can I get for you today?"

"The usual, Miss Ava." There's the ever-present wink. His tone is friendly, yet a hint of unwanted suggestiveness comes through, and I can't help the goosebumps that rise across the tops of my arms.

Not the good kind, either. There's no giddiness or excitement in me at his subtle flirting.

Instead, this man, with his average looks, light green eyes, and cheap cologne, makes me uncomfortable. It's like a blaring red light sits over his reddish head, and the moment he comes near me, it screeches to life to stay back.

I don't question the why. Far too many docuseries describing similar scenarios and the untimely end of those who didn't heed the warning exist, and I don't want to become a statistic.

Always listen to your instincts.

"Large black with no sugar and a half-dozen of our apple pie donuts coming right up."

"Thank you, Sugar."

"I'll be right back." I swallow down the demand that he quit calling me that—the urge to cringe—and succeed, but then a commotion comes from the kitchen. It's the sound of a loud yelp followed by a curse and then the screech of a metal pan hitting the floor. Eyeing the kitchen door, I sigh. Why me? *"Sorry about that. Your order will be ready as soon as possible."*

"Take your time." His chuckle meets my ears, and I turn to face him again. The smile he'd been wearing is now a cocky smirk, but it's the way Jason looks me up and down that catches me off guard. He's never been this blatant. Leering at me. "Seems to me you need a man around here, Ava. Someone to take control."

"I'm sorry?" My hackles rise, but with the bell sounding again and an older couple taking their place behind him, I bite back my unprofessional response for a second time. "I don't think I heard you correctly."

"Oh, you did."

Taking in a deep breath, I let it out slowly. Try to calm myself and my smart mouth. "Sir, I apologize if I gave—"

"We're going on a date this weekend." Not a question. A demand.

"Listen, I'm not sure—"

"Quit fighting me." Leaning over the counter, Jason lowers his voice so only I hear. Anger flashes across his expression, and I take a small step back. "We're inevitable, Sugar, and soon I'll own every single inch of you. That's a promise."

"Is someone there? Please don't hang up," the operator begs, bringing me out of the memory, and I nod, letting out a low whimper as another strike greets my ears. More pleas from this woman. His sick laughter. "Help is on the way, but I need you to find a safe location, and don't move if possible."

However, I don't listen. I can't find my breath and my chest aches—burns—as guilt threatens to overwhelm me. *Maybe if I'd reported him for the harassment this morning? Maybe if I didn't wave it off as just a man coming on too strong?*

Unbeknownst to me, I'm walking toward the house while clutching my phone tight. I'm close enough that the smell of spoiled garbage slams into my senses, and I crinkle my nose before pinching my nostrils closed. His community-assigned dumpsters are shut, but the funk coming from inside is stomach-churning, and breathing through my mouth doesn't lessen the smell. I move closer while questions flood my mind:

Why hasn't the HOA fined him for this stench?

Why hasn't anyone else called the police?

Where the hell is everyone on this street? In my community?

The grey home dead center on this cul-de-sac is where the noise comes from; I've seen this place a few times and have never given it a second look. It's nothing special. Just another large home with shutters and a pretty façade that blends in with the aesthetics of the area.

A familiar company truck sits in the driveway tonight, though, and my dread multiplies.

It's *his*. Why didn't I notice this before?

I'd know it anywhere, but before I can peer inside, a small flicker of light comes from a partially open window near the right side of the home. There's no gate or shrubbery to block my path, and I don't stop until I'm standing beneath it and rising onto the tips of my toes.

At once, my eyes close and the world becomes a muffled sound.

I'm afraid. Probably stupid. Not ready, but what if I can save…

Another blood-curdling scream. Another dark chuckle.

My eyes snap open, and the scene before me causes my throat to seize. There's so much blood, and the woman looks to be near unconsciousness. There are several cuts down her tied arms and torso —stopping an inch from her mound—and while they don't appear deep, her life's essence pools and then slides down her flesh in little rivulets of pain.

"Your life for hers. Consider yourself useful, my bitter little sugar." Bile rises, and I nearly double over as that term of endearment settles into me. It's a play on what he calls me…

Always sugar. Something to devour.

Keep it together, Ava. Put the phone a little closer so the operator can hear.

"Yes. You'll do just fine." Jason sweeps a blood-stained finger down her cheek before placing both hands at her throat. Her body thrashes, and everything around me comes back into focus—a sharp punch to my senses.

It's too much, and I scream.

The sound is loud and full of the utter fear coursing through my veins. Panic claws its way through my limbs, and his face snaps in my direction, eyes dark in the low lighting. His lips curled into a demonic sneer.

"Ava," he hisses and rushes toward what I can only assume is the front door. My eyes shift to the woman, and I see her chest still rising. It's slow, but she's alive, and that's all that matters. If I can keep him away until the cops… "Where the fuck are you, beautiful?"

"Get here quick, or you'll have two dead bodies," I choke on a whisper and take off toward the back of his home while giving the operator directions of where I'm heading. It's dark, and I can barely see, but I don't stop.

Jason's cursing and getting closer, his heavy boots stomping on the higher-than-normal grass as he makes his way toward the back.

With my phone still connected to the call, I light the way, stumbling over an old ax and lawn care equipment near the property line. I'm so close to the unoccupied lot behind his home—this is my only chance to escape—and I scramble over a riding mower to reach it. The unfenced parcel of land doesn't belong to our subdivision, and I'm so thankful for the wild cluster of older trees that provides cover as I crawl inside.

I don't care about the thorns scratching my skin; they sting, and I can feel a few drops of blood sliding down my arms as I move deeper inside and hide within the unruly shrubs.

I'm lucky that the faint sound of leaves rustling is masked by his heavy footfalls and the sudden rush of a scared cat running.

Large trees are up ahead, just a few feet away when he whispers my name, and I freeze.

"Where did little Miss Ava go? Come out, Sugar, and I promise to play nice after you ruined my surprise." His shoes crunch on old leaves or garbage—who knows—and I bite down hard on my bottom lip to keep in the whimpers that want to escape. I don't turn around, but I know he's very close. Jason takes another step, and his shadow looms near when sirens wail. They, too, are close, and he kicks something that sounds like metal near him. "You'll pay for this, and only after I've lubed my cock with your blood will I forgive you."

Oh God. Don't make a sound. I'm panicking as multiple car doors open and close; he doesn't move. The sound of Jason's front and back door being kicked in comes next, and someone yells for help—for an ambulance. Again, he doesn't move.

Multiple lights move throughout the backyard, focusing on him as feet pound the ground coming toward us.

He. Doesn't. Move.

But I know he sees me now.

How close he was to me.

"Hands up and drop to your knees," a man yells from behind us as multiple guns are cocked. Still nothing, but I feel him. His eyes burn into my flesh. Eating me alive. "On the ground now!"

At that moment, I look back, and our eyes lock a second before his knees are taken out from behind. He falls near me but can't react when three officers grab him and force his hands behind his back.

Jason is in handcuffs before I can blink.

He's being pulled up and searched as someone offers me their hand, and through it all, his eyes never leave me. Not once. There is no anger in them, either, which I find odd.

Instead, I'm given a disturbing grin. His cold, dark eyes are happy.

"You're safe," a female officer says, and my head tilts in acknowledgment. Through the corner of my eye, I notice her crouching down next to me, but I'm still trapped in Jason's stare.

"I-I'm. I—"

"Miss, are you injured? Do you need medical..." her words trail off then as I'm gripped by a horror-coated shiver running down my spine as Jason mouths the words:

"I'll come for you."

chapter 2

AVA

I'll come for you.

Four words, and they immediately wreak havoc on my nervous system; literal torture as I regain consciousness inside a sterile emergency room. Or was I admitted? I have no clue, and figuring it out takes a back seat as I remember the amused look in Jason's eyes while mouthing his threat.

I'll come for you.

The memory bombards me. As does the sick curl of his lips, and the disturbing expression begins thrashing inside my head on a constant, endless loop the more awake I become.

Repeatedly. Every horrific detail.

He's all I see until a light glitches, and I shift my attention toward the television mounted on the wall. The screen is black, on sleep mode, but at the bottom right, the date and time are displayed...

It's been more than twenty-four hours since this nightmare began.

I know I've been sedated. The initial shock after arriving and then panic attack, left the medical staff no other choice but to intervene via IV, especially as my nails clawed at my throat.

Because there's been no pause.

No reprieve. No forgiveness.

This haunting movie reel regains control over me as my mind feels split in two. I'm trying to reconcile my last memories after his arrest—his vile acts once again choke me—while slamming into my processors and simultaneously tightening an invisible noose that's slowly taking away my consciousness. I'm in and out of focus, once again unable to scream or ask for help, while the blood pressure monitor beeps loudly with my elevated distress.

While the world around me carries on as if nothing happened. As if an innocent woman didn't almost lose her life because of a demented man's obsession.

I'll come for you.

"He was proud. Smug." A truth that sends chills down my spine. It also takes me several minutes to mouth those words, a low whisper that hurts my already sore throat. Is it a lingering side effect of the medication they administered, or a byproduct of my reawakened distress?

I don't know, but I am aware of my surroundings.

Of each rapid rise and fall of my chest and the pain in my throat that reminds me of the time I had strep. Swallowing feels like a thousand shards of glass are tearing at my flesh, and I can't get enough air into my lungs. Each painful inhale stings more than the last.

My eyes do, too, as the tears begin to fall.

How can someone be so evil?

The answer, though, was clear in Jason's expression; his capture excited him. His satisfaction was palpable and suffocating as more of his depravity unfolded for the cameras to see, and yet, his biggest thrill of all seemed to be the part I played.

That *I* caught him. Exposed him.

"Good to see you awake, Ms. Perry. How are you feeling?" a female nurse asks, and I startle as she moves toward the multi-parameter monitor. She frowns at my reaction, but the expression deepens while looking at the readings. The blood pressure cuff begins to tighten then; it's uncomfortable, and the pain only serves to heighten my already chaotic pulse.

The result is higher than normal numbers. Even I understand this isn't good.

Everything feels wrong, and the understanding in her eyes is welcomed; I don't need to explain. She knows. In silence, I watch as she logs something into the computer system near my bed, taking in small, measured breaths that become my focus.

I don't want to acknowledge the feeling of fiery ants crawling under my skin.

I don't want to give in to the lashes of pain striking me from all angles.

"...we need to get your blood pressure down. This is too high." I'm not sure if she's talking to me or herself, but I give a slight nod anyway when she peers over at my face. Her expression is filled with sympathy as I remain quiet. She also doesn't comment on my lack of verbal response, which I'm grateful for. We both know I'm not okay. "I'll page the attending physician to order something to lower your blood pressure. In the meantime, would you like some water?"

I give another brief nod. The nurse props me up enough to drink from a straw—my hands are too unsteady to hold the cup—and she assists me with patience. The cool water is a double-edged sword; it settles my dry mouth while simultaneously causing discomfort as I swallow the three small sips.

Shaking my head, I manage a strained smile after she places the cup on a nearby table. It's taking everything in me to fight against the tendrils of anxiety crawling under my skin. To not give in and let them sedate me again, if for nothing more than to escape this purgatory.

"I'm going to leave this here in case you want more." Once the over-bed table is settled over my thighs with the cup within reach, she pats my hand and steps back. "You're safe, Ava."

You're safe. That's what the female officer who led me out of the backyard said, too, before several news channels descended on the scene. Each station set up seconds after the yellow tape surrounded the property, and reporters got as close as the authorities allowed…

Multiple voices called out questions while camera lights flashed.

Officers stood guard while making sure no one crossed the perimeter.

Who tipped off the press? I have no clue, but this is the kind of story that makes the national news, and each horrifying detail exposed makes everything worse.

For me. For the poor woman fighting for her life. For every victim.

Because I've been told this isn't his first time. That he's killed for pleasure.

"Were you not aware the community had an event tonight?" the officer asks, helping me sit down on the curb where a squad car blocks me from view. "Is there a reason you didn't attend?"

"Not tonight. There's something for next week." My voice is hollow as I shake my head. Hands shaking. "No one mentioned it today, either, at my shop. Or maybe I was too busy and didn't—"

"Breathe, Miss. Slowly in and out."

A sob lodges in my throat then, and my eyes become glassy as I stare into hers. "Ava."

"I'm sorry?" She's breathing in deep and exhaling slowly, gesturing with her hand for me to follow with an upward and downward motion, a movement I mimic as a jittery sensation starts at the soles of my feet and carries throughout my body. "That's good. Keep taking in slow, deep breaths for me."

Nodding, I continue the pattern a few more times before answering. "My name is Ava."

"Okay, Ava. You're doing good." There's movement to the left of us, someone rushing toward the ambulance while carrying a small object in his hand. The male officer hands it over to the EMT, and then the doors close. That truck takes off while the second one moves into the spot the previous one vacated; I know I'm next. That I need to be checked. "You were very brave."

"Doesn't feel like it." Tears fall down my face, and I feel as if a heavy weight sits on my chest, the pressure growing. "I should've—"

"No, Ava. You did the right thing by calling." Squatting down to my level, she grabs both my hands in hers and squeezes them. "She wasn't his first victim. He's killed before, and you did what others couldn't. You stopped him."

At the time, I was afraid to ask what they found inside his home for her to make that statement. And maybe I should've, but my focus once again turned to him.

While my world crashed, *Jason* enjoyed the acknowledgment.

He never tried to hide his face as he was escorted to another squad car, this one parked right behind his company truck in the driveway. Not when the door to the vehicle closed, either. Instead, he pressed his face against the glass and watched with that same sickening grin as the world learned his name.

I'll come for you.

"God, give me strength. Please help me get through this," I choke out a few minutes after the nurse left. This time, my voice is a little stronger as unbidden tears leave mascara tracks behind—I taste them. A sob also claws to escape my chest; I'm fighting to swallow it back with everything in me when I hear it…

The sound of a nearby television and my head snaps in its direction, eyes immediately locking on the entrance. My door is wide open, and with the layout placing me at the center of the room, I have some visibility into the one across the hall. From my position, I take in the man on the bed with a heavily bandaged arm and neck brace, the grimace on his bruised face, but that's not what makes me whimper.

It's not the blood, either.

It's *what* he's watching. What I *hear*.

"We're back with breaking news out of Dallas, Texas, where a suspect's in custody for the attempted murder of an unidentified woman. A neighbor coming home from work heard the victim scream and called the police, placing herself in harm's way to save the woman now fighting for her life at a nearby hospital. And as of the last hour, we can also confirm the accused is being tied to a chilling crime spree spanning multiple states. We now go live to our correspondent, Marcy Royal, in Dallas for the latest on this developing story."

"Thank you, Glenn. As we reported earlier, the sheriff confirmed that Jason Ripley, the man in custody, will be charged with the deaths of several victims. The deceased, all women and brunettes, were between the ages of nineteen and twenty-nine. These murders occurred over the last two years and stretch across several states. His arrest today brings relief to multiple communities on edge and could provide answers to a series of horrific murders that have shocked the nation."

"Marcy, what is our understanding of the motives? Do we have any information on what the boxes taken from his home contain?"

"We do, and the contents are disturbing, Glenn. There have been two shrines uncovered in the home's guest bedrooms. One to commemorate his victims, and the other, for the woman he seems to be obsessed with. The owner of a bakery—"

"Off. Turn it off," I beg through gritted teeth, and by some miracle of God, someone from inside the man's room closes the door. It provides me respite from having to listen to the living nightmare I'm trapped in—I'd asked the EMTs who wheeled me in to do the same when I first arrived. A different room then, but I'm thankful the nurse attending this one thought to do the same.

Right now, I prefer the silence while stuck inside this room, letting the strong scent of antiseptic burning my nostrils become my companion. Fear grips me, and by the look on the attending's face as he walks into my room a few minutes later with the nurse following close behind, hiding it is an impossibility.

He speaks, but I can't make out what he's saying. The cuff on my arm tightens again—it hurts the harder it squeezes, and the reading at the end is slightly more elevated than the last. They share a look, lips move, and when he shifts to give her what looks to be an order, I notice his badge holder clipped to his ordinary blue scrubs.

It's red. Bright red.

But more damning is the memory I'm hit with, this one more vivid than the earlier ones…

Jason holding a blade, the end dripping blood as he cut the young woman from just below her collarbones to her navel. Splayed open, the wound filled with her life's essence, pooling at the center of her torso before spilling over the sides of her bruised ribs.

So much blood everywhere. A surgically precise line.

I'll never forget the image or the sound of her pain-filled screams—the pleading to stop.

The gratification on his face while she begged for her life.

My mouth hurts, and I grimace as I try to unclench my jaw, but the pain is making it nearly impossible. I try to force out words, too, but fail. Then there are the alarms sounding from my monitors and the doctor's speaking to me, but I don't understand what he's saying.

Not that it matters a second later because the world goes black, and I finally find peace.

chapter 3

CRIME SCENE - DO NOT CROSS   CRIME SCENE - DO NOT CROSS

DETECTIVE FORD

Crouching beside a convenience store endcap, I place an evidence marker beside a butcher's knife with a bloodied tip. It's nestled against the metal bottom, almost hidden by a family-size bag of chips that fell as the robber crashed into the aisle while running toward the door.

Luckily, no one was hurt. Both the employees on shift and the customer buying cigarettes were unharmed, but the fucking idiot left behind a gift in the form of his DNA. This is the fourth store he's hit in East Hollywood, a series of burglaries that started a month ago.

The culprit is an older male between the ages of forty and fifty-five with a badly dyed beard; he made the mistake of looking up and into a camera on his second holdup while pointing his weapon at the female cashier. That day, it'd been a metal baseball bat.

He's changed his weapon each time.

A screwdriver.

A baseball bat.

A tire iron.

A knife.

He's growing more dangerous.

"But he's still a dumb fuck," I mutter, and Officer Baez to my left raises a brow, but I shake my head. "Not yet."

"We'll follow your lead."

"Good. No sudden movements, just keep actively searching this area." My voice is loud—carries—and those inside dusting for fingerprints or speaking to the victims call out a *yes, sir.* I'm not their boss, but these men and women know me—some have been part of the LAPD since I began—and they trust me.

No one acts suspicious as I take off my gloves and head toward the bathrooms. They're located near the soda and ICEE machines and are blocked by two large stacks of empty food trays that haven't been stowed away. The nightly food delivery came earlier than normal and before the store was robbed—the perpetrator's efforts have earned him a hundred and eighteen dollars and an upcoming arrest.

Because for some reason, criminals don't seem to understand that this type of business doesn't keep large amounts of money in their registers. It says so right on the fucking glass door, but he tried his luck anyway and won a one-on-one meet and greet with me in about five minutes.

There's a reason for the bulky steel safe.

There's a reason why every bill larger than a twenty is never held on to and deposited right away.

But they don't seem to teach that in the *how-to-be-a-shitty-criminal* class, and this idiocy comes with a very harsh lesson attached.

The suspect is wearing the same mustard-colored hoodie and

dark denim pants the store employee gave as part of his description. There's a new addition, though. A black bandana is wrapped around his left palm—his hand is clenched tight—and the hood from his sweatshirt is down, revealing a bald head.

Giving a subtle head tilt to Officer Baez, I stretch my neck while walking behind the counter and into the backroom. It's a quick deviation, but needed. The owner is talking with another detective near the designated office space, and both men turn and give me a questioning look. "He's outside by the mint green station wagon, lurking to see if we find anything. Get cameras on him. I'm going around back."

"You need me?"

"No. This one will be easy."

"Got him!" The owner pulled up the outside camera feed on his phone and turned the screen toward us. His eyebrows are furrowed, but a second later, he's glaring at the device. "I know this guy," he says more to himself than us, but it wouldn't surprise me. Most criminals visit their marks days, if not weeks, in advance. "He comes in every morning around eight and gets a medium coffee and two bananas."

"Every day? For how long?" I ask him while the other detective moves closer to the mop station. It's near the door, but the placement keeps him out of sight. "Did he come in alone?"

"Yeah. For about the last month, give or take." He nods, face pinched tight with anger. "I'm usually here by six to help with the morning rush, and you remember a customer after the third visit. I can prove it."

"Good. Get the video ready for us."

"And I'll watch the front from here. I've got a clear view." My colleague is new and has less than a year's experience, but the guy is dependable. Has a good head on his shoulders. "I'll put my parkour training to good use. He's not getting away."

With a nod, I head out the door with my cell phone pinned between my shoulder and ear. No one says or looks my way, but I make a jerky hand movement showing annoyance and move toward the small hallway where the emergency exit is. It's already propped open, has been since we arrived, and the forensics duo working tonight have already dusted for prints.

Within seconds, my phone is in my pant pocket, and I'm running around the side of the building. At the edge, I pause and look toward the station wagon where the culprit is still standing. He's fidgety, eyes staring toward the area where the knife was dropped while failing to blend in.

"Fucking idiot." In all the years I've worked in the LAPD, I've never seen a lazier criminal. I've dealt with cartels, gangs, and drugs to some capacity—assisted the narcotics team in dealing with cases attached to a homicide or assault charge of some kind. They go together. Repeat offenders escalate, and each offense is usually worse than the last, but this…?

He hasn't moved, much less looked behind him. Surveyed the scene.

Instead, the male is almost leaning against the car with its chipped paint and a sharp white strip across the center that makes it stand out, especially when parked close to a red Mercedez SUV and a newer model electric car.

Pulling my weapon from its holster, I make my way behind him. A few of the officers outside notice my move and begin to spread out, blocking possible points of escape—I'm a few steps behind him when a few bystanders turn their heads in my direction. It's a domino effect.

He does, too, and for a split second, his brown eyes widen in fear. Panic.

"Down on the ground," I shout while people scramble to get out of the way. "Now!"

Many rush away, their aim on the main street outside of the parking lot. There's one woman who's frozen, though. She's shaking. Her eyes are frantic and full of fear, but her body refuses to cooperate.

Son of a bitch.

The perpetrator notices, too. His hand twitches and begins to rise —she whimpers.

"Don't even think about it. On the fucking ground." I don't raise my gun, but his eyes flick to it.

"I'm not going back." He moves to grab her, his hand barely skimming her arm, when another officer yanks her away, and I rush forward. It's a split second later when my body crashes into his, the impact knocking the air out of him while his head bounces crudely against the pavement. Doesn't help that I'm fully adding my weight as I place my gun back in its holster and then grab my handcuffs. "Fuck, man. Fuck, that hurt."

His speech is a little slurred, but the man remains alert.

Doesn't stop me from securing cuffs on him, but once he's subdued and lying face up and groaning, I shout out to Baez. "Get him checked and, once cleared, booked. There's no blood, but he hit the ground hard."

"Head or body?"

"Both."

"Got it, Ford."

Patting his back, I turn to head back inside and wrap up my conversation with the owner when Baez says my name. Looking at him from over my shoulder, I notice his expectant expression and raise a brow. "Something wrong?"

"I expected for you to be a little more…"

"More what?"

"Check your phone." That's all he says, but when I make no move to do so, he shakes his head. "Captain Perez sent out a mass text fifteen minutes ago to everyone who worked the case. After the news broke out and—"

"What the hell are you talking about?"

"They caught the son of a bitch, Ford. Jason Ripley was arrested in Dallas a few hours ago."

chapter 4

AVA

It's been three weeks since that night.

Twenty-one days of tumultuous emotions running rampant inside of me; I'm constantly volleying from one extreme to the other as my once-peaceful life continues to disintegrate. From guilt to anger to a crippling sadness, I'm left with a heaving chest while this living, breathing nightmare continues to unfold.

I relive it from the moment I open my eyes until they close, and even then, there's no reprieve.

Because of Jason Ripley, I've lost it *all*.

My community. My shop. My peace.

Moreover, everyone knows who he is.

They've read about or watched the special news coverage of his crimes. There's a morbid fascination that's grown—people trying to get a glimpse into the mind of a serial killer while harassing anyone with information about his pending court case.

It's not enough to learn the details through journalistic accounts; I've been followed.

Cornered. Scrutinized.

My business was inundated with strangers trying to get a glimpse of the girl who *caught* him.

"Would you like to take a break, Miss Perry?" Silvia, the court reporter, asks while placing a bottle of water and a box of Kleenex in front of me. Tears are streaming down my cheeks, and I'm grateful for the gesture. She doesn't have to; her job isn't to cater to me or my emotions, but I appreciate it more than I can express. "It's almost lunchtime, and I'm sure both attorneys will agree that this would be a prudent time for a break. Or we can call it a day if you need?"

Her tone almost makes me smile. Almost.

She's a no-nonsense woman in her mid-forties with a navy blue and white polka dot knee-length dress, a beehive hairstyle, and bright red lipstick to polish off her look. It's cute on her. The style is a little demure meets sassy, while beneath the edge of her white cardigan, I see what looks to be a dragonfly tattoo on her wrist.

She's made this deposition a little less everything:

Uncomfortable.

Anxiety inducing.

Stressful.

"Thank you…" I muster a wobbly grin and shake my head "… but I'd like to get this over with. Like a Band-Aid."

"Still going to call it for lunch, Ava," she says, and two male voices agree with her through the video conference call. The district attorney and the defense both move to disconnect the meeting, but I hold a hand up in the universal stop motion.

"Is something wrong?" the DA asks while the defense looks at me intently. "Would you like to call it for the day, instead? We can reconvene tomorrow morning?"

Taking in a deep breath, I let it out slowly. "How much longer?"

"Can you be more specific?" The District Attorney closes the notebook he'd been jotting down notes in. His eyes hold empathy.

"How many more questions do you have for me? Both of you."

"I don't have anything else, Miss Perry." That came from the defense attorney. He's been quiet for the most part, and over the last two days, he only asked one question... *Do you have any physical or mental impediments that affect your ability to observe or remember the events?*

That's it. One simple yes or no question.

His defense is based on my credibility as a witness because of the documented panic attacks I had at the hospital. And yet, he failed to read deeper into my medical history, which clearly states the trauma of witnessing his client's horrific crime slammed me into a state of shock and then utter fear.

Not during. Not while I was running for my life.

After, my emotions weren't mine. I became a prisoner of the circumstance and couldn't control it.

He also didn't ask why I was there. Why was I walking home from my bakery that night?

My answer to his inquiry was a resounding *no* because I remember every last detail.

This isn't my first rodeo with this investigation, and after going through the events of that night multiple times, I'm not the slightest bit desensitized. There's no forgetting. No way to bleach his stomach-turning smirk from my memory.

My recap of the events before, leading to, and after haven't changed, either.

Not when the detectives asked for my initial recollection and then my formal statement. Not when I picked Jason Ripley's picture out of a lineup of twenty, and after the administrator wrapped up the procedure, I spoke to the head investigator again.

Over and over, and not once has my account of the night changed.

"We've gone through the night of the attempted murder and then his persistence in asking you out." The DA picked up his water bottle and took a deep sip before placing it back beside a chain-store coffee cup. "But we haven't discussed your earlier ties to the accused."

My brows furrowed, and I shook my head. "I have no ties to him."

"You went to school together, Miss Perry. Do you not remember—"

"What do you mean we *went to school together?*" It comes out a bit shrill, and I slip my hands to my lap, clenching my fingers tight. Breathe in deep to try and calm my racing heart. "No. That can't be right. I'd remember if—"

"From our investigation, we uncovered he attended the same high school as you. Jason was a senior during your freshman year at Twin Rivers High."

"B-But I don't remember him at all." *He has to be wrong. Has to be.*

"Noted." His eyes shift away from the screen for a second before flicking back. "How about the name Anthony Salcedo?"

"My old neighbor?" The DA nods, and the defense writes something down, but neither says another word while I swallow hard. I remember him. The guy one of my closest friends had a huge crush on. *What happened that year...* "He was on the baseball and soccer teams...always nice to everyone. Huge manga fan, too."

"How do you know that?" This time, it's the defense lawyer who chimes in.

"Because he spent hours at the same comic book shop one of my friends worked at." It wasn't my scene, and I never really visited the place, but Rose never stopped gushing about him. "She was sweet on him, but he never really noticed her. Not the way she wanted, anyway. Anthony was busy spending his time between sports and hanging out with two other guys from our school, but I never paid too much attention to them."

"Why not?" the DA asks.

I shrug. "Didn't want her to think I was attracted to him. It's girl code."

Both men let out a low chuckle at that, but it's the prosecution that responds. "Understood. I've got twin daughters in college now, and I've heard it all. To be honest, they scare me a little bit."

If he was trying to make me laugh, he failed, but it did pull a small smile from me. "We can be ruthless…"

"I plead the fifth here."

"Smart man." This segue from the truth smacking me in the face calms me a little bit. Enough that I'm able to exhale slowly, and the constricting feeling in my chest eases a bit with each breath that follows. "But to answer your earlier question, I don't remember him. Not the other guy, either. They mostly kept to themselves. Didn't hang out with others—no clubs or school activities. Anthony was the only trio member who stood out. Popular and nice, most of the girls in our school liked him, especially after he took the baseball team to state, and they won."

"Would you happen to have a yearbook still? Or access to one?"

Before I can respond to the district attorney, Silvia, taps her watch. "We need to call it. Miss Perry and I deserve some food and fresh air."

"Agreed. But I'm going to request we end her deposition here." The defense sits forward and meets my stare through the screen. "Miss Perry, thank you for your time."

"You're welcome." What else can I say? Can't tell the man simply doing his job to go fuck himself for defending a despicable animal because no human being would torture and kill innocent women for pleasure.

"Good day." He exits the cyber meeting, and Silvia holds up a finger, making sure he's disconnected and the log-in passcode changed. It's not the first time I've seen her do this. She's been in charge of everything—from recording the deposition via an old-school tape recorder, to documenting every word in that short-hand typing they do. There's also her kindness toward me—going out of her way to make me as comfortable as possible.

"We need to wrap this up, Devin. I'm hungry." There's a coyness in her eyes, and he smirks for a second before shaking his head.

"Forgive my wife. It's our anniversary, and she wants to duck out early."

Wait." My eyes volley between the two, and they couldn't be more different. She's vibrant to his subdued. Sassy to his serious. "How is that possible? Should you be working on the same case? Will I get you in trouble?"

"Not at all, Ava. Everyone in the state knows," Silvia says and then laughs. She also winks at me. "We're nothing if not professional, and I've been known to hand him his ass more than playing nice. The fact we can argue in here and then go home and enjoy a bottle of wine just makes it more special."

"Okay." There's nothing else I can say to that. To be honest, having seen her navigate, and, at times, intervene when I became distressed, endeared her to me. I would've never guessed, and at the same time, it makes me smile. A genuine one for the first time in so long. "That's lovely."

After a few seconds of silence, her husband clears his throat. "Do you have that yearbook by any chance?"

I shake my head "No. Sorry." My head tilts to the side, and I run through the select few people I've kept in contact with over the years, wondering if anyone has a copy. "Except for my senior year, I tossed everything out."

"That's okay. We'll contact the school and—"

"But I might know someone who might have a copy. I'm almost positive she never tossed any of them away."

"Rose?" Silvia asks, her brow arched. "You said she had a crush on him."

"No. We're not on good terms anymore." That is the understatement of the century. She changed after we graduated, or maybe it was before. My best friend pulled away from me and became defensive after the position she put me in. "I'm talking about another friend. If anyone has a copy, it's her. Amanda worked on the yearbook community and helped put them together, including the year you're asking about."

"How soon can you reach out and explain our urgency?"

"Today. Why?"

"Because I have a limited window to turn in my transcripts," Silvia interjects, her expression serious now. "Everything you just shared will be given to the defense, Ava. I won't hide anything, but the fact he exited the meeting before everyone is in your favor. Devin getting his hands on every piece of evidence and building a solid case will make sure Jason Ripley isn't let off based on a technicality or lie."

chapter 5

CRIME SCENE - DO NOT CROSS CRIME SCENE - DO NOT CROSS

DETECTIVE FORD

This is a fucking mistake.

That thought runs through my mind—a nonstop loop of forewarning as Captain Perez explains my next assignment. Fifteen years older than me and at one point a marine, he's someone I respect and have never questioned, but this time…

I'm receiving the bare minimum while he pushes a sealed file across his desk that I haven't opened yet, but the longer I sit here, the more my irritation mounts.

This has to be some kind of joke.

I'm not a hired guard on duty, much less a roommate's babysitter. Not that it *can't* be asked of us: certain cases require round-the-clock protection, but this precinct has never demanded it of its officers. It's a sign-up detail, the time given with incentives, but not like this, even if it is for a case that leaves a bitter taste in my mouth.

"She'll be under your watch until he's caught and sentenced," Captain Perez says as if sharing the weather report and not the bullshit job I've been assigned to. "We need her in that courtroom, Ford. Her testimony alone will put him away for a very long time, if not the rest of his life."

The *him* is a serial killer.

The same son of a bitch I've been chasing for over two years.

A murderer who somehow managed to escape captivity during a routine transport a few days ago after his initial hearing in Dallas.

"This bullshit…" I run an agitated hand through my short hair "…wouldn't be necessary if they'd just handed him over like our district attorney wanted. It started in Los Angeles and should end here. Those three families—*all* of those girls—deserve equal justice and not to be an afterthought."

"I agree, but Texas as a whole has a larger body count than us and won the toss. Nothing I can do since California was denied the right to extradite and process."

"Then send me back out into the field. You know I'm a bigger asset hunting the sick son of a bitch down than watching over her," I beg through clenched teeth. "I can find him. I know how he thinks."

"That's why you'll be a bigger *asset* to me here. Protecting her."

"I'm sorry, Capt., but I don't agree with you." Keeping my eyes on his, I bring a bottle of water to my lips and take a deep pull. He's my superior, and I need to remember that. No matter how hard I want to knock some sense into him with my fist, I can't. "Everyone—every single person that worked this case wants this man's head, but we're being blocked because of a back-door compromise between states. A few shaken hands and a promise of recompense later decided Texas would charge and process while attaching our victims' names to their already thick file. Each murder—thirteen in total—will now carry the maximum allowed. Am I correct?"

Captain's jaw ticks. "Yes."

"That isn't enough, and you know it."

"And what would you like them to—"

"He should die." Plain and simple. "That's a fitting punishment."

"Trust the laws you serve and protect, Ford. He won't get away."

"He already did, and it's been a week," I manage to say while biting back the colorful variations of the word *fuck* I want to add between every few words. "His victims will never hug their families again. They'll never have a chance to get married and have kids of their own, and instead of bringing their memories justice, we've let them down. The possibility of a larger body count rises each second he's—"

My phone vibrates inside my pocket then, cutting me off. I'm glad for the small break in conversation; I need to get ahold of myself if I'm going to get out of this assignment. Pulling it out, I see it's a text from my mother, but I don't open it, choosing instead to put it on vibrate as I school my expression.

Mask how the guilt eats at me every single day that bastard is on the run.

Those bodies haunt me. Every life taken could've been prevented had I caught him.

However, after a year of following leads that led me to just within reach, he disappeared out of sight. Not a single trace for months. It's as if the ground opened up and swallowed him, hiding the son of a bitch, only so he could reappear in Dallas after leaving another string of deaths at his heels between three large cities.

Texas. Arizona. California.

Perez exhales roughly, running a tired hand down his face. "We found another body that matches his M.O., and this death is being added to his grocery list of charges." *This is a motherfucking mistake; I should be out there hunting.* "... and because of this, Ava will be staying with you in your apartment."

Those words stop my train of thought, and my eyes refocus on Captain Perez. *The fuck?* "Sir, I don't think I heard you right. Repeat that one more time."

He can't be…

Fuck. No.

"You did." He picks up his coffee cup and takes a sip before sitting back in his chair. There's an edge of exhaustion in his tone that matches the dark circles beneath his eyes. His accent also thickens the slightest bit, which is not noticeable to most, but after working together for so many years, I can pick up the Spaniard inflection. "Take that with you and study it front to back; it holds new sensitive-to-the-case information that few are privy to. I trust *you,* Ford. I know that you'll keep her safe no matter the cost. She's too important—the only person that can identify him from that night."

"Can't Meyers or Anderson take this instead?" I try one last time. "I'd be more useful—"

"I want you alone to handle this. Very few people…" he points at me "...know of her whereabouts outside of the ex-military guards driving her across state lines. They've already been instructed to deliver her to your home within the next six hours, Elijah, and we'll be keeping it that way. End of discussion."

"From Dallas?"

"Yes."

"Why not a transport from our precinct?"

"Because she's been in their protective custody since Ripley's arrest." Perez's expression and tone are angry, almost matching mine. "They've kept her guarded while the state prepared for his trial, an advantage since I know people in her city."

"Is there something I'm missing? It doesn't sound like the HPD is on her protection—"

"I asked two ex-Marines for help." *What the fuck?* "And before you ask, this is both a favor from the two men *and* a concession the Texas DA had no choice but to make. I've known them for years—since their fathers were rookies—and they are trustworthy. More than passed the state's vetting."

"This feels personal, Captain. Why are you getting to choose where she goes?" *Why my home?*

"There's a nationwide manhunt." That's all he says. No further explanation. Perez evades the first question, and for now, I let it go. Choose to fight a different battle.

"We don't know if he's heading this way, sir. *He* doesn't know she'll be here."

"Unfortunately, we have reason to believe Jason has a tracker on Miss Perry. Someone is trailing her movements from within. That, and all departments are stretched thin looking for this asshole."

"Then plant a decoy and send her far away. Alaska if necessary." We know how this goes. The extremes to which officials will push themselves to catch a criminal, even using one of our own as bait if warranted. "This wouldn't be the first time—"

"That's a territory I have no leverage over."

"What does that mean?" There's an icy edge to my voice, and I flex my jaw to keep in a few expletives. "I deserve a better answer than that."

"It means, Elijah, that we do our job and keep that girl safe," he says, matching my tone. The bottom of his mug cracks as it meets the edge of his wooden desk, and what's left of his black coffee spills and falls to the floor. "You are my best detective and someone I trust. Prove me right."

"Understood." Because nothing I do or say will change her coming here. So, instead of losing my temper, I grab the file. Flipping open the first few pages, I read the basic information on the perp again—because I know him—and at once, that same rage I experience when dealing with every homicide case fills me.

Only this time, there's an added tinge of unease, but it's overshadowed by the need to kill him myself. It's been growing for a while. Since he escaped our grasp because a dead criminal can't hurt anyone, and I've more than made peace with that.

He doesn't deserve to live.

- **Accused: Jason Ripley**
- **Age: 28**
- **Born: Tulsa, Oklahoma**
- **Occupation: Supervisor at a small lawn company.**
- **Lives: Dallas, Texas (Prior address is from Los Angeles, where he resided for eight months and then moved back while evading the LAPD.)**
- **Currently Resides: Two streets from the witness's home. (Shrine found inside a guest bedroom with pictures of Ava Perry in various scenarios: some in public, others in the privacy of her home, and a few are intimate.)**

Reading a few more pages, I take note of the obsession Jason has with the victim under state protection. There are highlighted sections of his interview after his arrest: threats and the hoarse growls of her name detailed by those who witnessed his capture.

Each report is almost an exact copy and paste—the new details giving me a small glimpse into her living nightmare—and a weight settles on my chest. Guilt eats at me.

It's probably why Captain Perez chose me; he knew I'd take it personally. Knows I'd do anything to stop Jason from killing again, and his hard-on for this young woman means she's both a target and his destruction.

She'll be the cause of his downfall. That one mistake all animals like him make.

Because crimes of passion are sloppy and desperation leads to reckless choices.

Closing the folder, I sit back and meet his hard stare, fighting not to show the ire flowing through my system. I'm still angry, but this time it's for a woman I've never met. How we've failed to protect and end this nightmare for her and any possible future victim. "They have to know he's desperate, that he's coming for her in a place he's familiar with. Jason having lived here and escaping our chase gives him an edge."

His nostrils flare while nodding. "Yet on the same note, it has a few advantages. The first is the detective who almost caught him and knows how he operates." Perez opens the top drawer on his right and pulls out another folder. This time, it's in red. "That's what makes you the only person I trust with her life."

"I still don't like it—"

"Noted." Perez lifts his brow while tapping the red file with his pointer finger. "He has to travel through a few states and evade a lot of people, including you, to get to Miss Ava Perry. Those women —*all* those young lives taken—deserve justice, Ford. And this is our best chance to do just that."

Nodding, I scratch the two days' worth of stubble on my jaw. "They're going to need all the manpower available to track him down. Jason Ripley is conniving and resourceful; thinking this capture will be easy is a mistake."

"Agreed." A moment of silence follows. He seems to want to say something else but remains quiet, and I take that as my cue to leave. There's no point in arguing anymore. Once he makes up his mind, it's set in stone, just the same as I won't rest until Jason Ripley's dead or behind bars by my hand—

The only acceptable outcomes.

Rapping my knuckles twice on his desk, I push my chair back and stand. "I'm out."

I make it a few steps. The handle of the door is just within my reach when Captain Perez clears his throat, and I stop. I don't turn around but tilt my head to the side so he knows I'm listening.

"I chose you for a reason, Elijah." A heavy sigh follows. "Keep her safe. Nothing else matters. No matter the cost."

chapter 6

CRIME SCENE - DO NOT CROSS CRIME SCENE - DO NOT CROSS

DETECTIVE FORD

She's his muse.

"That sick son of a bitch," I grit out, grabbing the file I'd pushed away a minute ago. My fingers clench and unclench, renewed anger coursing through my veins as I lean over and begin flicking through the pages. I'm seeing everything through a different set of eyes, taking in the details not as the detective who hunted this animal down, but as a victim. "How didn't anyone make the connection sooner?"

All women. All young. They were between the ages of nineteen

and twenty-nine with the same physical attributes: chocolate brown hair, blue eyes, and were short in stature.

Jason saw Ava in every victim. Substitutes he used and killed to ebb his obsession with her. And as I read through each line, I'm cataloging the moments of pure fear she must've lived through, instead of analyzing *him*.

The torture of not knowing what will come.

The survivor's guilt all victims carry.

Then, there are the questions I've come to expect as part of the healing process while interviewing the parties involved with murder cases.

It's a wash, rinse, and repeat cycle as I read through the notes Dallas detectives, a psychologist, and their district attorney added to the thick file. I'm numb to it for the most part unless it pertains to her answers. Something about this woman invokes this near-painful need to—

Protect. Avenge. Bring peace back to her life.

The reaction wars against the reality of a man like me: numb to the ugliness of the job.

Drugs and assault or trafficking—murder. Not because I've lost my humanity, but because a clear head doesn't make mistakes. Attachments cloud judgments. It can place innocent people in danger, and that goes against my oath—my badge.

Pinching the bridge of my nose, I exhale roughly and then stretch my neck. The area feels tight, I'm tired, but there's little time left before Ava Perry arrives. "She's just a case. Nothing more." Picking up my cell phone from beside an empty soda can, I press play on the audio file Captain Perez sent me after our meeting. I've listened to it more than five times now, always pausing at the fifteen-minute mark:

"Do you have any questions for us, Miss Perry? Anything we can do to help the transition into witness protection more—"

"There's nothing that will make this easier or less horrifying, Detective." No one says anything, but a tiny sob slips through, and the sound causes my chest to ache. Her voice is low, a tiny whisper, but I find myself attuned to it—to the most minute hitch of her breath and the utter fear in her tone. ***"Nothing but his capture will heal me. Will bring some semblance of safety back."***

"We'll do everything we can, Miss Perry."

"That's all I can ask."

If they notice her lack of trust, those in the room don't comment, and a few seconds later, they begin to discuss her transfer. She's coming from Dallas to Los Angeles with a private escort set up by my precinct.

She's been thrown into an unknown situation with variables out of her control. With no one she fully trusts.

Asking herself if she'll ever be safe from him.

Wondering when she'll go back home and what she'll walk into.

The woman's been moved two times since Jason's arrest, the first due to the harassment. People who knew her spoke out in interviews, exposing who she is, and the amateur paparazzi began to press her for whatever details she knows and that the media isn't sharing. Then, they inundated her bakery, made it impossible to run the business, and followed her every move through the lens of their cell phones.

Then it happened again, once he escaped police custody during a transport trip.

It's a lot to take in for anyone. Fucks with their head.

Closing my eyes for a few seconds, I focus on the soft breeze coming from the open balcony doors. The scent of salt water has always soothed me—lulls me into a state of calm where I can think rationally.

Page after page, it's full to the brim with notes on both of them. His fascination with her is plain to see within every line—morphing into a sick obsession the older she becomes. My mind pulls to the forefront a few details that stand out from the file…

***Ava went to school with the accused. Three years younger than him, they didn't run in the same circles, but he was close friends with her childhood neighbor, Anthony Salcedo.**

***She ran into him again as a customer at her shop. He came in daily after the first encounter: 7 a.m. (February to the end of September) ordering the same thing: black coffee with a half-dozen apple pie donuts.**

***Asked her out on a date consistently, which she turned down politely. Over the last month, he increased his insistence from once a week to an almost daily occurrence; Jason was demanding the day she caught him. Miss Perry reported his last words to her that morning as follows:**

"We're inevitable, Sugar, and soon I'll own every single inch of you. That's a promise."

***The first body was found a mile from her home after the first refusal: a twenty-four-year-old brunette he picked up at a bar and choked to death. Examination of the body concluded that there was no sexual assault, just physical.**

"How old was she when his obsession started?" a thought that forces me to take a metaphorical step back and analyze *how* no one noticed. Who's helping him?

That's when Perez's words from earlier crashed into me. The tightness in his expression gave more than the sternness of his command; it was a plea. A warning.

"Very few people know of her whereabouts outside of the ex-military guards driving her across state lines. They've already been instructed to deliver her to your home within the next six hours, Elijah, and we'll be keeping it that way."

"Ava Perry?" I whisper her name aloud, opening my eyes just

before the doorbell rings. A few seconds tick by, and that ring becomes four quick raps against the wooden surface. They're loud, but not as annoying as the continuous pressing of the doorbell. Standing, I grab my gun from the coffee table and make my way over. I'm more than halfway there when whoever is on the other side knocks again. Inpatient or in a rush to...

My eyes shift left to a clock on the wall, and I realize just how much time has passed since coming home. Two hours where I've been lost inside my head while reworking the puzzle pieces this case brought to my door.

Another knock. Softer this time.

I don't look through the peephole, though, knowing it's her, and pull the door open. The problem with that; I didn't think things through. I'm not prepared for what greets me, and in that minuscule second where my eyes meet a pair of light blue ones, I curse Perez for my destruction.

I'm caught. Can't look away.

My eyes scan her face, memorizing everything from the freckles over the bridge of her nose and cheeks, to the small scar over her right eyebrow. It's tiny, a crooked line partially hidden beneath the hair there, and I find it *cute.*

Lowering my eyes, I settle on her plump mouth. Its natural berry color is appetizing, even more so as this tiny beauty bites down on her bottom lip while looking up at me through long, thick lashes.

She's simply gorgeous. Blushing.

The blood throbs within my veins and my cock hardens; it pulses with each rise and fall of her chest. With the way, her own eyes look at me with curiosity.

"Detective Ford?" she asks, and as those lips slightly pucker at the end, I know why I've been feeling off. Why I knew taking this assignment was a mistake…

AVA

MY LIFE WILL NEVER BE the same. How could it be?

I've gone from owning a quaint little café to being on the run. From having friends and a life of my own to absolutely nothing in the blink of an eye because I was given no choice but to disappear.

There were no goodbyes. No last hugs. Nothing.

Taken from my home in the middle of the night, I was told to cooperate and follow instructions. To simply go with two men I don't know, and trust that they'll keep me safe until we reach my next handler a few states away. This is the second time I've been moved in the past few months: from Dallas to San Antonio and now Los Angeles with nothing but empty promises that this will all be over soon.

This is the loneliest I've ever felt.

Not even when my parents died did I feel so isolated. For my safety, I'm being kept hidden from the public eye and the plethora of hungry reporters vying for an exclusive I'll never give. Then, there are the morbid fans following every printed snippet while making up their own theories on the case.

Some are right. Some are way off.

And I can't blame them either. How many times have I watched crime documentaries and put the pieces of the puzzle together in my head, finding angles that others never thought about? It was my way to unwind: a glass of wine and some pizza while a gruesome story unfolded, often without criminals seeing the inside of a prison cell at the end.

It was when the letters and emails began—I was being followed around—that my protection detail removed me from my safety net.

My bakery. My home. My routine.

I've been stored away like an object in San Antonio where his trial was set to begin, but then he escaped. Their mistake is why I'm being driven to Los Angeles without a choice in the matter.

Three states. More bodies. And more than one life was taken by this monster in each.

The more his depravity comes to light, the more I realize it's my fault. His obsession isn't new; it began when we were teens. I didn't pay attention to him now or knew he existed back then, but the truth is, he hurt those women because I turned him down.

A monster with a wounded ego. I've never told a soul how uncomfortable and pushy he's become. About the one time he—

"We'll be there shortly," Jaime says from the passenger seat while Adam nods. The all-black F350 is roomy, and I thank God because the last thing I want is anyone close enough to pat my hand. It's a short statement like all the others before; they're not rude. Not in the least. Jaime's tried while Adam is the silent type, speaking only when necessary.

They don't work in law enforcement. Taking on this last-minute responsibility of protecting me until we reach my next handler is a favor, and one I'm very grateful for.

I no longer trust anyone in Texas.

Moreover, I know Adam's disposition has nothing to do with me and everything to do with the beautiful blonde he kissed goodbye before we got on the road. Jaime's goodbye was more subdued, but watching them—their love and how tender they treat their women—made me think of what I'll never have.

Not for a while. Maybe never.

Not with the fear that grips me tight at the knowledge that my worst nightmare could be anywhere. Maybe following in the car behind us. Jason could be biding his time so he can take from me what I never gave him willingly.

"Thanks. Can't wait to stretch my legs," I say, trying for enthusiasm and failing miserably. My palms are sweaty, and I wipe them down my denim-covered legs while pretending to clean something off. "It's very pretty here."

Adam meets my eyes through the rearview mirror and nods. "The detective in charge of your protection lives near the water. We could stop there first if you like. Get some fresh air?"

"That's very kind of you, but I would rather we just get this over with." I'm sure the smile on my face looks more like a grimace, but he's kind enough not to mention it. Neither of them do. My nerves are choking me, the worry almost making me sick.

It's been four days since Jason escaped police custody, forcing the change in game plan. We've gone from lying low to a secret race in which very few are participating in. From conviction to recapture while playing a game of hide-the-witness.

It's also brought back the nightmares; a horrific movie reel that never fails to keep me awake.

Her screams. His laugh. All the blood—

I'll come for you...

"You'll be okay, Ava. Safe here." Adam sounds so sure of himself that I don't have the heart to tell him how much I doubt that. That at this point, my hope is almost gone.

"May the good Lord hear you," I mumble and then refocus my attention on the passing scenery. My eyes shift every few minutes, looking at the cars passing us and praying that Jason isn't in one of them. Some shoot us a quick glance, but most continue to drive as they maneuver through the busy traffic this state is known for.

And they weren't lying. California is everything you see on television: lively, busy, and beautifully scary because it represents the unknown. I don't know anyone here. I'm alone.

Jaime lowers his window, and then Adam follows, lowering the rest to let in the salty, fresh air coming off the nearby water. It's gorgeous—a warm shade of bluish green that soothes me, seeping deep into my bones.

Closing my eyes for a second, I take it into my lungs and sag against the seat as the ex-Marines drive me toward the detective's home. For a little while, I let go and regain control of my anxiety—I pretend this is a vacation and not a forced seclusion.

I don't know how long I stay that way, but a hand nudging my shoulder pulls me from my semi-relaxed state. "We're here." Jaime's voice is low, while his expression is one of concern.

"Thanks." Taking my seatbelt off, I exit the truck while taking inventory of my surroundings. The building before me is huge. Intimidating. And yet, as we enter the fancy lobby and get on the elevator, there's no fear. Instead, the same sense of calm that settled over me as I took in the fresh saltwater scent, enveloped my tired limbs tenfold.

It catches me off guard and makes my knees a bit weak, but I stay quiet. Maybe it's the exhaustion taking over or the repercussion of my lack of appetite, but when we get off on the twenty-fourth floor, I have to force my legs to cooperate. One foot after the other, I follow a quiet Jaime down a long hallway after making a right turn while Adam remains downstairs, grabbing my bags.

At the very end, Jaime stops in front of a door with the number seven on it and tilts his head in my direction. "You ready?"

"As I'll ever be."

"For what it's worth, Elijah Ford comes with high praise and is familiar with this case. If anyone can keep you safe, it's him. Trust him." My mouth opens to reply, to tell him that I've heard this from someone I *do* trust, when his phone pings with an incoming text. Jaime snorts after reading it and looks at me. "Adam needs help with the bags. Be right back."

"No…" he walks away before I can finish, pushing the doorbell on his way "…problem."

For a few seconds, I stand there, and…nothing. So, I knock. Hard.

I don't like being out in the open like this, and my escort has disappeared around the corner, so I pound my fist a couple of times to make sure I'm heard. It takes a few harsh knocks from me and the push of the buzzer for that door to open, and when it does, what I find is a thigh-clenching and naughty-dream-inducing specimen of masculinity.

Lord, have mercy on my soul. Amen.

chapter 7

CRIME SCENE - DO NOT CROSS CRIME SCENE - DO NOT CROSS

DETECTIVE FORD

"D*etective Ford?"*

Christ, she's beautiful. Those pictures in her file and on social media didn't prepare me for the stunning brunette standing before me with blue, innocent eyes and lush lips. For the way my body reacts to her curves, and I feel like a right asshole for it.

For being attracted to the woman I'm meant to protect, not fuck into the nearest surface.

This is the last thing she needs after what she's been through.

"And you must be Miss Ava Perry," I manage to say, fighting back the need to move closer, and yet my voice still drops into a husky cadence as I taste her name on my lips, a soft touch of pink grazing the apples of her cheeks.

Fuck me. This is bad.

"Yes." Her lids close and her chest expands, rising and falling with each deep inhale. She's nervous. Maybe a tiny bit intimidated. Unsure. However, that doesn't stop her from doing an exploration of her own. Right before they shut, her gaze sweeps over my face and then lower, down my broad shirt-covered chest and then stomach…

I can't stop the clench of my abs, nor the way my cock gives a jerk beneath the confines of my sweatpants, something she notices, and the hint of heat that flashes through those baby blues is proof of how fucked up this is.

It's why she's refusing to look at me now.

This sudden attraction is mutual. Palpable. Tempting.

She needs my protection, not my dick. Don't make her uncomfortable.

Even as I repeat that mantra, my feet carry me closer without permission, aching to touch her. Comfort her. Tell her that everything will be okay, but I stop just before the heat coming off her skin seeps into my bones. Before she can innocently test my control.

Instead, I bring her sweet scent into my lungs and then take two steps back. It rocks me. Makes my mouth water, and I swallow hard while fighting the pull.

Son of a bitch, what is wrong with me? After this is over, I'll kill Captain Perez myself.

Fuck old age getting to him.

My eyes take in her body—posture—the way she cocks her hip on the right and how her tiny hands clench. She doesn't move for a few minutes, not so much as a tiny shift, and it isn't until I clear my throat a few times that she looks at me. "Where's your luggage?"

"Down in my truck," one of the two men walking toward us answers, stopping a few feet from a quiet Ava. My reaction is immediate, and I move past her, reaching for the gun tucked into the waistband of my pants, but the gleam of dog tags makes me pause.

The I.D. tag on the one who spoke reads Jaime Suarez; he's tall, muscular, and giving me a grin that borders on cocky as he holds out an overstuffed book bag. As if he's privy to information I'm not. "Nice to meet you, Detective Ford. I'm Jaime…" he points at his friend "…and this is Adam."

"Elijah, and likewise…" I trail off, knowing nothing of this man past the fact he's been responsible for Ava up until this point. *She's my responsibility now.* Someone I'll protect from a lunatic stalking her. Nothing more than another case.

Jaime extends a hand for me to shake then, and I do before his eyes shift over to the woman standing beside me now. "And I believe you've already met Miss Ava."

"Not exactly."

"Why is that?" Adam asks, his brow arched, eyes shifting between us. "Is something wrong?"

"Better yet, why was she left alone on my doorstep?" Because that deserves an explanation. It's more important than my sudden attraction for my temporary ward, even if we both know she's completely safe here. More than the conflicting thoughts running rampant through my mind, because now isn't the time to decipher what it means.

I want to hide her inside my home and wrap her in a cozy blanket, shielding her from the world. And in the same breath, I want to lay her down across my bed and part her thighs before licking—

Ava holds a hand up, her cheeks still that delicious rosy color. "Jaime ran downstairs to help Adam with my luggage, Detective. I wasn't alone."

"Call me Eli," I interrupt, my eyes back on hers. It doesn't go unnoticed by me that I'm also asking her to use a nickname I hate. "Please."

"Okay, Eli." Christ, the way my name sounds coming from those pouty lips is indecent. Provocative. Another mistake on my behalf. *Keep it impersonal.* "I wasn't alone, though. You were here, too."

Jaime coughs something under his breath, and his friend nods, breaking our moment. Both men are looking at Ava, but it's the former who speaks. "Why don't you come help me bring your things up? We'd like to have a word about—"

"Sure."

"No," we answer in unison. A mistake on my behalf because their subtle grins become full smirks at my flat-out refusal to let her leave. Jaime is enjoying it much more than his friend, but they're amused, nonetheless, while I'm becoming more tense by the second. "I'll go."

Because beneath the relaxed behavior meant to assure Ava things are going as planned, I've caught Jaime's jaw ticking every few seconds. Then, there's the way his partner's body is positioned to keep track of anyone coming onto this floor.

There shouldn't be any foot traffic as I own this section of the penthouse level, something they should be aware of. Two of my three neighbors are on vacation, while the last spends most of his workweek running a software company out of Silicon Valley. This is one of his many properties, not the home base, and is used to entertain or unwind with his flavor of the month.

Something is wrong.

"I don't want to stay up here by myself, Detective." Ava looks perplexed by my reaction. A little annoyed, and it's a welcomed sight. There's still some sass in her despite the nightmare she's navigating through. "Besides, I need my stuff. Promise it's not much, and—"

"I'll get them for you."

"But—"

"Go inside, sweetheart." *Son of a bitch.* The term of endearment slips past my lips before I can stop it. Jaime opens his mouth, and Adam tilts his head to the side while she just looks at me—I carry on as if I'm not tripping over myself. "I need to have a word with them. We'll just be a few minutes."

"Actually, that might be best," Adam adds.

After giving them a quick nod, I smile down at her. "We'll be right back."

"Are you sure?" Gone is the blush and embarrassment. Now, there's a hint of panic in her voice, and my heart clenches. Assuaging Ava's fear will be my new priority.

Extending a hand toward her, I wait until warm fingers slip between mine and walk us inside my condo, ignoring the Marines. We don't stop until we're outside on the balcony overlooking the Pacific Ocean. Standing side by side, our eyes survey the beauty all around us:

The busy city. The water. The clear blue sky.

And it's in this moment of silence, fingers intertwining, that her body loses its rigidness. That she let out a shuddering breath, and her lips quirked up into a soft smile full of relief. "This is beautiful."

"It is." Nothing more is said for a while. Could be minutes or hours; I wouldn't know as my focus stays on her. How she breathes in deep and then exhales slowly, calming herself. She's fighting against the small bout of panic that's trying to take her under.

Her fingers in mine are a bit sweaty, but no longer clinging tight. Instead, the stiffness slowly becomes languid, and her mild shaking stops the longer we just stand here.

At that moment, the phone inside my pocket vibrates, and behind us, the front door closes softly. Yet, instead of turning around to look, I take out my phone and read the text from a number that is familiar from the case file atop my coffee table.

I'll bring her things up. ~ Jaime S.

Thank you. ~ Ford

"You probably think I'm being ridiculous," Ava says from beside me as I pocket the cell phone. Her voice is low, a gentle hum.

"Not at all." Studying her profile, I take in just how beautiful she is. How delicate her features are, from the small button nose to her pouty lips—she's what I imagine a living doll would be. "After everything you've seen and endured, I expect you to panic. Not trusting your surroundings and the people in it *is* normal."

"I feel safe here, though," she mumbles, and it's almost too low for me to hear, but I do. The confession causes a weird sensation to overtake my chest, and I rub the spot. There's pride mixed with confusion and…*want*.

I want her to need me.

I want her here.

Christ, Ford. Get a hold of yourself. "I won't let anything happen to you, Miss Perry. You're safe inside my home and with me. All I ask is that while Jason's being hunted, you don't go out alone. Please don't put yourself in unnecessary danger."

"I won't, but I have to ask—"

"How long before we catch him?"

"Had you let me finish..."

Her mock glare pulls a chuckle from me. "My apologies. Go on."

"Thank you." Ava pushes a dark, wayward strand of hair behind her ear while a slight blush once again spreads across her soft cheeks. "I was going to ask you about the security of the building?"

Good girl. "No one gets in or out without a key, and the staff knows to I.D. those without one. Of course, visitors come and go, but they are vetted and approved by the residents through the onsite security."

"So, no strays?"

"No." Extending my arm toward her line of sight, I lift my wrist so she can see the app at the center of my smartwatch. "This alerts me to anyone standing at the door, and on my phone, there's a live feed of the same. So even if I'm not here, I'll be able to see and come right up."

"That's a confusing statement."

"I use the gym downstairs and at times, the conference room." Tapping the app on the screen, I show her the camera's view. "I'll keep you safe. Promise."

"To serve and protect…right?" The way she words it causes me to lower my arm and fully turn to face her. Placing my hip against the balcony's veranda, I study the furrow between her eyes and how her shoulders hunch a bit.

"Does that bother you? My oath?"

"It's the same one officer after officer fed me back in Dallas, Elijah. Each time I gave my accounts of the night, picked him out of a line-up, I was made that promise, and they all fell short time and time again."

"I'm not them."

"You're also human."

"And so is he."

"He is." She's facing me now with an apologetic expression on her face. Ava's silently asking me not to take what she's saying personally. "But it hasn't stopped him yet. No one's been able to—"

"You doubt me?" Because that wouldn't work. I'll do whatever it takes to help her find peace again. "What can I do to ease your mind?"

"No. And nothing." Ava bites her bottom lip and looks away at my raised brow. I hate it. Need that sweet gaze back on mine. "And that scares the hell out of me. I don't know you, Elijah, but this is the first time in months that there's a small kernel of hope that this will all be over soon."

Without conscious thought, I bring a hand up and cup her chin, tilting her face up to mine. Blue eyes meet hazel, and there's a hint of something dangerous in her stare. For me. For her.

Because that yearning—the hope reflecting back at me—will be our downfall.

This isn't the time to start anything.

Under different circumstances, I would've asked her out. Explored this undeniable attraction.

People meet every day and start something new within minutes, but this time it's wrong. She's forbidden fruit as my temporary ward, and nothing—not my cock or need—come before this case.

Keeping her safe is all that matters.

"Explain, sweetheart," I ask, my tone low as my thumb strokes her cheek. There's a hint of heat from her blush, and the pink is so tempting. *So pretty.* "Why does it scare you?"

"For some inexplicable reason, Eli…I believe you." Ava nuzzles my palm once and then pulls back as if burned. She's shocked by the act, but at the same time, takes my hand in both of hers, and the soft skin cocoons mine. I feel as though I'm being burned. Just a simple touch sets me ablaze, and it takes a herculean effort to stay as I am. To not kiss her. To not feel her. *She needs your protection and nothing else.* "…I feel safe inside your home, and that can end badly for me. A few minutes out on your balcony has done more for my stability than every breathing exercise I've been taught. More than the armored military escorts."

"You deserve security and peace." Ava's words don't make a lick of sense, and I know my expression mirrors the thought.

"Complacency will get me killed, Detective. We both know that." Ava lets go of my hand and steps back, an invisible wall replacing her warmth. Those baby blues are sad as they watch me. "I'm afraid, Elijah. I've seen what he's capable of."

"I'd kill him before—"

"He's coming for me." Those four words hold nothing but acceptance, but before I can respond, a knock comes from the front door. We step apart as it opens. Jaime and Adam walk into the living room, their hard gazes finding mine while mirrored serious expressions mar their faces. They are downright pissed the fuck off.

Three quick vibrations also alert me to a missed message, and I know it's from one of them.

"Give me a minute," I say, already walking back inside. Something went wrong, and leaving her alone on the balcony for the time being is the best choice. Whatever it is, I don't want her to hear it just yet.

I'll break it to her after I know what I'm dealing with. Much later, once we're alone.

"He's—"

"Outside, now." My voice is harsh, body tensing as I make my way outside the apartment, not stopping or making sure they're following me. Instead, I walk toward the center of the floor, where there's a small sitting area overlooking the bay not far from the bank of elevators. It's far enough to talk without her hearing—but there's also a large enough mirror where I can see who's coming and going —and I can reach my door within seconds if need be. "Tell me."

"There's a new victim."

"Fuck." It's a rough exhale as I drag a hand over my face. "Female? Where?"

Adam nods, his lips in a thin line. "This time, the body was found in New Mexico. There's also a note."

"What did it say?"

"See for yourself." Adam hands me his phone, and my eyes scan the picture; I begin to shake. Pure fucking lava courses through my veins. On a white sheet with a smattering of blood is a single line written in black marker:

You can't keep her from me.

The plastic in my hand groans, and I hand over the device before it becomes a thousand pieces on the floor. A million scenarios run through my mind, each one worse than the last as the marine takes his phone back, and I shift my eyes toward the water not far from my building.

It's a little choppy at the moment. Growing violent.

Matches my conviction. My truth.

"I'm going to kill him."

chapter 8

AVA

Elijah walks away without looking back.

But more importantly, I hate how that makes me feel. Alone. The worry slams back tenfold.

This crippling fear I've been swallowing down—fighting back—unleashes as memories flood my senses. They're hitting me full force in the chest, and I have to grip the railing tightly to keep myself upright because his facial expression said it all: confirmed that this new reality isn't changing anytime soon.

There are two things I'm also certain of:

Jason's coming for me.

Something's happened since we left Texas.

A bitter truth to swallow because…

I can't look at Elijah as anything other than the man ordered to protect me. I can't focus on his hypnotic hazel eyes or the way my heart thumps rapidly when they settle on mine. Or how his over six-foot, muscular frame makes me feel delicate and safe. How my fingers itch to run through his thick, wavy black hair and pull on the ends to see if he groans.

The horrible timing of my attraction to him isn't lost on me, either. Any sane or normal person wouldn't be thinking this way; they'd be afraid of their own shadow, but those few minutes when our fingers intertwined soothed the frantic emotions swirling inside of me. We can never be, but that doesn't stop me from taking him in and reveling in the warmth his honeyed eyes provide.

Maybe if this was another place and time…

I can't let the butterflies inside my stomach, the ones that dance and make me hyper-aware of his every move, lower my guard. Taking in how handsome he is isn't conducive to staying alive. It's the opposite; Elijah could be put at risk if I get too close.

"No one around me is safe. It's all my fault." That causes a small sob to catch in my throat as my vision becomes glassy. I'm the reason for a madman's cruelty, and I cannot handle another death on my hands. "My life will never be the same."

Nor is it fair, but I have to get ahold of myself.

Even thinking about getting close to the detective—or any man—is a mistake and isn't healthy in my state of mind. I'm not okay. Recognize it.

But more so, because Jason won't let me go.

He told me as much…

You'll pay for this, and only after I've lubed my cock with your blood will I forgive you.

A harsh shudder runs down my spine, and I grit my teeth. Breathe in and out as conflicting thoughts wage a war inside my head. I'm safe for now. I'm angry at myself, the latter of which for being stupid enough to ignore his advances.

Why didn't I acknowledge how creeped out he made me feel instead of pushing it aside, pretending that Jason was just another pushy male? The kind that thinks persistence will get them the attention of a woman who doesn't see him in the same light?

No one owes it to anyone to appease their ego.

No matter the gender. A person's sexuality. Or religious belief.

No means fucking no. Period.

I still failed, though, because I didn't speak up. What if he knows I'm here and...

"You're safe. No one can get in," I whisper on shaky legs, my chest rapidly rising with every harsh intake of air. Standing is becoming too difficult, and I slide down to the floor. Turning with my back to the veranda, I lower my body with my knees bent up and take in a few deep gulps of air, limbs shaking.

The world around me is a muddle of sounds.

I'm scared, and time seems to move around me while I'm stuck inside my head. And yet, when a pair of arms pick me up and hold me close, everything comes back to me.

The noises. His sandalwood masculine scent. A warmth that settles deep into my bones and calms my panic.

"Elijah." It leaves me on a breathless whimper, and his arms tighten around me. My head is nestled against his chest, and I'm matching my breathing to the sound of his heart beneath my ear. It helps me focus.

"I have you, Ava. Just breathe for me." The chill of his A/C hits my skin, and I shiver, burrowing deeper. Eli walks a few steps further into his living room and stops, turning with me in his hold, and sits. I'm astride his lap, clutching his shirt while his hand, the skin a bit rough, runs up and down my back in slow motion. I should feel fear, especially after Jason, but I don't. There's no discomfort, either. Instead, the warmth coming from his body seeps into mine. "That's it. Slow and deep…match mine."

Up and down, the touch is gentle as his chest expands, and I mimic the move. For a while, we just sit there, in the quiet of the late afternoon, breathing. He doesn't rush me, and I don't want to move from his embrace.

Rather, I soak up his attention. Enjoy what I can't allow myself to want.

"Better?" he asks a few minutes later. His lips are on the crown of my head, just lightly pressing there.

"Yeah." My voice is a bit hoarse, and my throat is dry. I'm thirsty, and he picks up on this.

Elijah's quick to pick me up and set me down on the couch beside his now empty spot. "Be right back," he calls out over his shoulder, entering another room that connects to this one.

Immediately, I miss his warmth. How good he felt against me. How safe.

Christ, I need help. Something can't be right if...

I hear a cabinet door and then the fridge open right before a crash. The loud sound makes me jump in my seat, and I find myself rushing toward him on still-weak legs. I'm feeling the aftereffects of my anxiety, a bit lethargic now, but I can't stop myself. "You okay in there?"

"Yes." There's a muffled curse, and another item falls. Glass this time, and it shatters. "Just peachy." He sounds grumpy, and maybe even a little bit cute, as he tries to hide whatever's happening. However, nothing could prepare me for what I encountered upon entering his kitchen.

It's comical, to say the least.

"How the hell?" A giggle slips through my lips, and his head snaps in my direction. The expression on his face is one of annoyance, but it quickly softens as I take in the hot mess he's created. "Again, Eli. How?"

A large Tupperware container full of spaghetti and meatballs is spread about everywhere, splashed on the walls, cabinet doors, and the floor. On top of that, there's broken glass and what I think is lemonade from a pitcher.

I take another step inside the kitchen, but he holds a hand up, stopping me. "Watch your feet," he grunts, his tone a bit harsh a second before glass crunches beneath my sandals. Bits spread out further, one or two jumping on my toe. Eli sees this and lets out another low *fuck* before marching over and picking me up.

His hands on my hips pull a gasp from me, and goosebumps spread across my sensitive skin.

I shiver. Clench. Almost whimper.

Why does he affect me this way? Like no man has before.

For years, I lived and breathed for my shop. No dates, much less time for a relationship. Time and time again, I would say "no" to Jason—and anyone who asked me out—choosing instead to fixate on the new sales promotion and flavors for each month.

I focused solely on what I could create inside my kitchen to entice my clientele.

Besides, while I've never slept with a man or woman, I've owned a few vibrators over the years. My suction cup dildo does the job of taking care of my needs, although technically, some might still consider me a virgin even if I am stretched to accommodate my eight-inch toys.

No fumbling or nerves. Just me at my own pace without any outside pressure.

I've been more than content to fully take care of myself. To be alone.

I'm not a prude. I've just never been interested enough to try. My toys are faithful, always give me orgasms, and I don't have to worry about somebody's schedule or job.

Something tells me he'd be worth the ride...

"Where did you go, beautiful?" Elijah says, bringing me back to the present. I'm sitting in the middle of his island now, legs slightly spread, with him standing almost between them. And I say almost because even though his upper body is leaning toward me, his hips stay a few inches from my knees. Close enough that I feel his heat, but not touching. Even his hands stay away from my flesh.

He keeps one on each side of me on the counter, palms face down.

"Nowhere?" It comes out as a question, and he raises a brow. "I just spaced out."

"Don't lie." My face heats up, and he smirks a bit. "Share with the class."

"Just thinking about the mess you made. How dirty you are?" Something flashes in his eyes; they darken a bit at my words, and my blush deepens. "I meant your shirt. You have stains...not that you're dirty, as in…*sexually*."

He chuckles. I'm becoming flustered, and he knows it. "You don't say."

"*Christ...*" I throw my hands up, almost knocking him in the chin. "I'm talking about the room. Not you. It's filthy in here."

"Quit while you're ahead." His voice is a bit huskier. Almost smooth like chocolate.

"I'm done now." Crossing my arms over my chest, I lean back, avoiding his stare. Once more, I take in the grimy surfaces while ignoring his presence—how easily he distracts me from my earlier panic—and it's while I look around the room that a few things stand out…

My luggage and my military escorts are missing.

"Your bags are near the entrance. Jaime and Adam had to go… something about one of their wives."

"How did you know what I was thinking?"

"Not that hard when you whisper those thoughts out loud." Eli is a bit smug, and I do something that's completely out of my norm. I flick his forehead, and hard. Hard enough that he jumps back a bit and narrows his eyes at me.

There's a split second between my hit and Elijah wanting to retaliate, but before he can, I jump down from the countertop and walk around him. The space between us is something I need.

To think. To clear the fog he creates.

To continue ignoring just how easily he makes me forget my troubles—my fear.

"Where are your cleaning supplies and mop?" I ask while surveying the room once more. More glass crunches beneath my feet as I walk around him and toward his fridge. It's even worse over here, and the food is drying, becoming gunky against the stainless steel of the appliances.

"I'll clean up after you leave the kitchen."

"No."

"No?" He sounds as though he finds my response amusing.

"That's right. I said no." Turning around, I face him with a hand on my hip. His lips quirk up into a full grin. "What do you find so amusing, Ford?"

At the mention of his last name, Eli licks his lips, and I unconsciously do the same. "Stubborn little thing, aren't you?"

"Not at all." Sassy. A little challenging. *Why am I so comfortable around him after knowing him for less than a day?*

"I find that hard to believe." He takes a step forward.

"Quit changing the subject." Matching his actions, I take one back and then another. Eli advances, and his eyes are predatory, something that should send me running, and yet, it doesn't. It's thrilling. He's taken my fear and replaced it with a feeling of euphoria that's confusing and, even more worrisome, welcomed.

I can't. Shouldn't. Moreover, I want it. His attention.

"You're not cleaning this, Ava. Go to the living room and wait for me."

"I'll get this tidied faster than you," I say a bit breathlessly. Then, because life needs to remind me of just how wrong this is, I take two steps back, bumping into the counter area beside the fridge. A mistake that puts a halt to our flirtation—this moment—as a coffee cup tips over, rolling onto the floor beside my feet, where it shatters into a million pieces.

My reaction is to scream and jump. To think the worst.

Elijah is across the room and has me in his arms before I can blink. Cuddling me to his chest, his lips press against my forehead. "It's just a cup. Nothing happened."

"I'm sorry."

"Don't," he growls low, hugging me closer. Comforting me. "You could break everything in here, and I wouldn't care. Do you hear me?"

"Yes."

"Did you get hurt?" Not that he waits for my reply; the man kneels at my feet, looking for any visible cuts.

"No, but I am more embarrassed by my reaction." Heat blooms across my cheeks and to the tips of my ears. "Can we just drop it and clean up? Please."

He makes a sound at the back of his throat, a mixture of a grunt and groan that forces my eyes to his. "You hungry?"

My stomach rumbles then, and the blush heats further. "A little."

Eli raises a brow from his position, head tilted to the side. "When's the last time you ate?"

"A real meal?"

"Yes."

Pursing my lips, I recall our stop just outside of Dallas to pick up a late dinner and shrug. "Two days ago."

Once again, I am lifted onto a countertop, which pulls a squeak from me. This time, though, he doesn't linger. "Stay," is all he says before leaving the room for a few minutes. When he's back, there's a mop, broom, and a bucket in his hands, along with a few rags.

Placing them near the sink, he opens the cabinet below and pulls out a few spray bottles with different-colored liquids inside.

"Can I help?"

"After I sweep up the glass." And that's what he does. Broom in hand, he gathers the larger pieces, picks them up, and tosses them inside the garbage bin. Then, after nothing is left besides the small bits, he begins to sweep the floor clean of spaghetti and glass.

Watching him work like this, doing something so domesticated, is...*sexy*.

Tempting me with what I shouldn't want.

A house.

To share my life with someone.

To not run or constantly have to watch my back.

Elijah Ford is going to be extremely dangerous for me.

"How about now?"

He looks over and rolls his eyes with mock annoyance, sweeping the last bit into a dustpan he produced out of nowhere. Or did he bring that with him? "...dirty. Can you?"

"I'm sorry. Can you repeat that?"

"Can you wipe down the appliances and cabinet doors that got dirty?"

"Oh, um. Yeah." I brace my palms on the granite to help me jump down when, in the blink of an eye, he's on me. Grabbing my hips in his strong hands, Eli picks me up and places me on the floor right in front of him. I stumble a bit and brace myself against his chest. "Thank you."

"Just don't want you to get hurt. These are higher than the standard because of my height."

Our proximity is like a drug, clouding my judgment once more. And before I can chicken out—before I can rationalize just how idiotic I am—I lean forward and kiss his chin.

That quick peck on his skin nearly breaks me in two.

However, because I'm a bigger chicken than an idiot, I step back quickly and avert my eyes, focusing instead on the different bottles beside the rags. "Which one can I use for the cabinets?"

"Either of the two light pink ones is fine." It comes out as a groan, and I ignore it. Choosing to focus on the task at hand, I fight the urge to turn around and let him see me.

How he's affecting me.

How much I wish it'd been his lips instead.

This man is the epitome of tall, dark, and handsome, with the words *wrong time* stamped across his forehead. There's also something completely lovely about how easily his clumsiness breaks down the last dregs of my anxiety. Because right now, as we work in tandem, I can't help but smile and ignore the slow ache building through my limbs.

This moment is honest. Sweet. Just what I needed to feel a bit normal again.

chapter 9

AVA

I'm a wimp. Can't deny it even if I wanted to.

Not when I've gone out of my way to stay out of sight for four days now. If he enters the room I'm in, I leave, finding every excuse under the sun to avoid meeting his stare for longer than a few seconds.

To keep from drowning in his *everything*.

It's the only way to survive him. Us. This attraction is wrong—forbidden for more reasons than just his job. His assignment is to protect me.

My focus should be on surviving Jason's threat and staying alive, not on the detective keeping me safe—even if he embodies everything I find attractive in a man.

He's strong and protective and thoughtful, and *fuck me* if he's not handsome. Sexy in a way that makes my breath hitch and my palms sweat whenever he's close.

It's a weakness. A temptation.

To not fall for him? I flee.

To not lick his jaw? I hide.

Like now, I'm standing in front of the door to my room contemplating my next move: head outside or stay? Offer myself, or disappear?

Stop. Breathe. It's nothing and will stay nothing.

Not that simple for two reasons:

I'm attracted to him.

And my predicament leaves very little in the choice department.

I need clean clothes. Desperately. However, avoiding the temptation he represents makes a commonsense problem difficult. Especially when he's kind. Generous. When he goes out of his way to anticipate what I need and doesn't bring attention to my neurotic behaviors.

The small amount of clothes I grabbed in my rush to get on the road with the military escorts is now dirty, and I'm down to my last pair of panties. I've avoided this long enough, and as I glare at the door, I breathe in deeply to quell my nerves.

That flutter of butterflies that suddenly appears when I see him.

"Get out. Do laundry. Come back," I whisper low, hand shaking as I turn the knob and pull. Suddenly, the *Mission Impossible* theme song plays through my mind, and I stifle a giggle at my ridiculousness. Here I am, tiptoeing out of the room while looking around like an idiot and shielding myself with the laundry basket Elijah was kind enough to leave for me.

Dear God, I've become certifiable.

Heading toward the small closet near the kitchen, I take notice of his office door being closed and pause. It's a first. *Is he in there?*

That's also the moment I realize there's no noise—no sign of *him*...anywhere.

It's disappointing and a relief all at once. It also makes me wonder just where he is.

Elijah's always here, working or sitting out on the balcony watching the tide come in every evening. It's a ritual, watching him from the entrance to the living room and out of sight, taking in the sharpness of his jaw and the bob of his throat as he sips a tall glass of iced tea.

It's the most serene I've seen him. Calm and fucking beautiful.

"Where are—what the hell is that?" I whisper-shout, almost dropping the basket in my hand. There's a deep and sudden rumble, followed closely by the *thud* of something hitting the floor. And even though I shouldn't, I follow it. It takes me to just inside the living room, where I stop because what greets me there messes with my system.

With that internal clock, all women have.

Elijah Ford is here. Asleep on his couch. He's holding on to a throw blanket in his left hand while the other hangs off the side with a phone on the floor beneath his fingertips.

"Christ, please help me," I say low, a prayer, as a tiny snore slips past those lips. Lips I'd give anything to kiss. To taste.

I can't stop myself, either. I'm not in control of my body. My feet carry me to him, almost close enough that his fingers brush my skin. Almost.

It's reckless.

Stupid.

But I don't care. The pull between us makes me do what I shouldn't, and while I know I'll regret this for days to come, I gingerly pull the blanket from his hand and cover him. There's a sigh from his lips, and something mumbled—an unintelligible grunt—that quiets into a hum of approval when I kiss his forehead and then chin.

The feel of his skin on mine sears me. Destroys more of the wall I need to keep erect.

For a second, I close my eyes and savor him just like this. In secret. Privately.

Without him knowing that I had a moment of weakness.

"Sleep, Eli. I know you're tired."

"Stay, Ava." Every cell in my body freezes, and I'm afraid to look at Elijah and find him staring up at me. Of being caught. "I'll protect you."

Those words cause my eyes to flash open, and I realize he's dreaming. Thinking of me. Of being my hero. *I'm screwed* because this unconscious act endears him all the more to me. These emotions growing within are a torment. Unfair.

Why couldn't I have found him in a normal setting?

At the movies. My bakery. Or even a grocery store?

We could've bumped into each other while on vacation, like all those movies I love to watch while curled up under a fluffy blanket on a cold night. Because without a single doubt, I know I would've let myself get swept up in him if I had.

With that thought in mind, I walk out of the room and toward his laundry area. I'm on autopilot as I do, putting my clothes in, setting the temp and load size, and after dropping in some detergent, I close the lid slowly. Elijah doesn't stir, and I don't go back to where he is.

Instead, I slip inside my room and close that door.

I don't lock it, but hide behind the four walls just the same.

It's better this way. No one will know about my moment of weakness.

No one but me.

I'M RUNNING, prickly branches scratching my skin as his laughter slithers down my spine. He's close. Too close, and a sob catches in my throat as I push past another rusty lawn tractor in my way. There are too many of them; it feels as though this maze is sending me in circles while Jason toys with me.

"I promised I'd come for you, Sugar. We're inevitable." Jason's voice skims the flesh of my ear, and I scream, throwing an elbow back, but there's no one there. Instead, I'm met with the sensation of something cold sliding around my ankles, nearly making me trip, but when I look down, I find nothing but deformed hands coming up from the ground with extra fingers attached. Different shades of skin. Different shapes and lengths. They claw at me with chip-painted fingernails, burrowing into my legs until rivulets of blood stain the grass below. "Come to me, and this will all stop."

"No. This can't be real," I whimper right before I'm yanked by the ankle and stumble, my hands bracing my fall. Tiny rocks cut into my palms, the sting making me hiss as the fingers drag me across the ground.

I fight and kick. I dig my hands into the ground and try to pull my body forward, but then a pair of black boots appear in front of me.

I'm afraid to look up.

The leather is wet and sticky; a pungent stench greets my nose, making me heave. I'm trying not to think about why the shoe is that way, but fear makes it impossible to wrench my body back. Instead, I'm unable to stop him from forcing my chin up and head back until our eyes meet.

Jason's are pitch black, like what you see in horror films. The smirk on his face sends chills down my spine. "I warned you, Sugar. You'll pay for this, and only after I've lubed my cock with your blood will I forgive you."

"This can't be real."

"But I am, Ava. I'm your nightmare and future." His shoe moves from my face so he can squat down, my body within his reach, but he doesn't touch me. Jason's hands are clenched at his sides while the sudden blare of a siren gets closer. Just like the night of his arrest, his face transforms into one of relief. "I did all of this for you. Why can't you see that?"

Multiple car doors open, and then there's the heavy vibration of footsteps coming our way. It's déjà vu as guns are drawn and voices shout—I can't make out a single word they're saying—but I am *trapped by his expression.*

The evident relief of being caught. Of no longer having to hide from society.

"I'll come for you."

With that declaration, he allows me to see the darkness inside of him.

His obsession.

His desire to hurt me.

He reveled in my fear.

Once again, I find myself drowning in that same sickening feeling as the night of his arrest. His body hits the ground so close to mine that I feel his rough exhale against my cheek—the manacle around my bleeding ankle disappears—and a small cry breaks through my lips.

I'm trembling and failing to find purchase on the ground and move away when a warm set of arms wraps around me…

"I got you, sweetheart. You're safe." The voice is familiar and warm, doesn't scare me, and I find my consciousness being drawn to it. "That's it. Open your eyes, Ava. It was just a bad dream."

Every bit of me wants to; I find warmth in his soothing voice, but…

The horrific memories replay on repeat, and I can't *unsee* them. It's a living, breathing horror flick I'm stuck inside of. Over and over. Never pausing or giving slight relief, I'm left withering under the sound and smell—so far away, and yet I feel every vibration. Every sharp note in his vengeful promise resonates and claws under my skin, and while I'm not a hundred percent sure if it's real or I'm imagining it, it shakes me just the same.

Right now, I can't make the distinction to save my life.

Am I stuck in a nightmare, or is this my real life?

How can I go from being a happy bakery owner to witnessing such a crime? But then again, nothing makes sense, and the world around me continues to tremble uncontrollably.

A sob shakes me, and the strong arms holding me tighten, the soothing scent of mint and sandalwood with a hint of saltwater that's uniquely *his* overtakes my senses. It's the best of both worlds; the forest meets the ocean in a way that's not overpowering or obnoxious —just him.

"Good girl." Elijah's deep baritone continues to break through my racing memories. It has to be a nightmare if he's here and assuring me that I'm okay. "Come back to me."

I whimper, and the sound hurts as I try to open my eyes. "Eli—"

"Yes. I'm here." His arm around my waist maneuvers me until I'm closer, and my back meets his chest. In this instance, there's nothing sexual about our position, even if we've never been this close before. This is about comfort, and when he lays a tiny kiss on my temple, I open my teary eyes and look back at him. "There you are."

He lets out a relieved sigh and I can't help but shiver, a bit from the lingering effects of my dream and partly because of the man holding me close. As if I'm precious. Important to him.

Don't overthink it, Ava. Elijah's just being empathetic.

"I saw him, Elijah," I say, voice rough and shaky. "He promised to come for me."

"Nothing and no one will hurt you again, Ava. I'm here." A promise and conviction, and for some reason, I believe him, even if I fear Jason just as much. It's what I'm clinging to as my body loses some of its rigidness and my breathing becomes even. One of Elijah's hands runs soothing circles up and down my arm; he also waits until I'm a lot calmer before speaking again. "Do you believe me?"

"I do." Honest and without hesitation.

"Then let me be here for you. I'll keep the monsters away." Another kiss, this time on my tear-stained cheek. "Sleep knowing that I'll protect you. That I'm not leaving you."

Snuggling against him, I bring the comforter up to my chin and exhale shakily. I'll worry about propriety later. Right now, I need this. To not feel alone. And maybe it's my exhaustion and the late hour, or simply because I feel safe in his arms, but it doesn't take long for me to be lulled by his warmth.

Even between layers of clothes, I feel him. He's all muscle and comfort.

"You promise?" My voice is low. Almost a whisper.

"Yeah, Ava. I do."

Nodding, I close my eyes as the last tears fall. I breathe him in and exhale slowly. "You'll stay until I fall asleep again?"

"I'll be here when you wake up."

"Thank you." A bit slurred now, but his chuckle against the back of my head tells me he heard me just fine. Eli's response to that comes through as nothing more than a rumbled grunt. I'm sure there are words in there somewhere, but sleep has taken over.

Yet, one word comes through right before it all goes black:

"*...mine.*"

chapter 10

CRIME SCENE - DO NOT CROSS CRIME SCENE - DO NOT CROSS

DETECTIVE FORD

Son of a bitch, it was a mistake, but I couldn't help myself.

Not when every inch of her body calls to mine. When I'm attuned to the smallest noise she makes and her every smile. The real ones and the fake ones, because to me, she's an open book with a never-ending story I want to read.

Today and tomorrow.

Ava Perry calls to me in a way no woman ever has, and I fear that once this case is closed, no one will captivate me as she does. We met under the worst circumstances, and yet, I wouldn't change it.

Even if I can't have her the way I need her.

"I'm truly fucked over this sweet little morsel," I whisper against the crown of her head, nuzzling her soft skin while she sleeps in my arms. I haven't left her room, and I won't, no matter how hard I am —the way my cock throbs with every rise and fall of her chest— because right now, it's not about me. What matters is her comfort, not the aching of my balls.

I never want to hear her cry out like that again.

The way she whimpered out a "*no*" and "*this can't be real*" earlier tonight broke my iron-clad restraint. I couldn't sit in the living room, a repeat of an earlier basketball game playing on the TV, and not react to her distress.

I moved toward her room without a second thought, my body thrumming with anger at the asshole who caused her nightmare. My fingers turned the knob, pushing open her door before I could stop myself, and the thrashing sight before me ignited every protective instinct within my DNA.

Fuck not crossing the line. Nothing but soothing her mattered when Ava's sweet face was pinched tight in distress, her comforter pushed down past her knees, and tears slipped from beneath closed lids.

"He'll pay for your tears with his life." Her head turns in my direction as if she heard me, and those luscious lips part on another whimper. The sound causes my chest to ache, and before second-guessing myself, I'm lying on the bed and tucking her close. We're both fully clothed—this isn't meant to be sexual—and I'm ignoring every carnal need she evokes in me, especially when she fits perfectly against my harsher planes.

Her being in my arms feels right.

Truths I ignore while coaxing her into fully relaxing. I'm running my hand up and down her back in soothing strokes, placing tiny kisses across her forehead and taking her decadent scent into my lungs. She smells like my favorite dessert: raspberry crème brulé. It's caramelized sugar with vanilla custard and a touch of brightness in the raspberry that's simply perfection on her. Mouthwatering.

I also feel a hundred feet tall when she trusts that I'll protect her.

My heart thumps harshly inside my chest when she asks me to

stay until she's asleep. It doesn't take her body long to give in to the exhaustion, melting into my comfort, but I make one more promise before she's completely under.

The words are honest. I don't regret them, either.

Much like she took care of me earlier today when I napped on the couch, the feel of her soft lips pulling me awake without her noticing, I'll watch over her. I'm giving her a piece of me, even if I know we'll never have more than this. Ava Perry will always have my loyalty.

Without trying, in a short amount of time, she's burrowed herself under my skin.

I'm constantly thinking of her. Wanting her close.

"Sleep knowing I'll watch over your dreams. I protect what's mine."

chapter 11

AVA

I've become the master of *evasion*…

My life. The case. Wanting Elijah.

Just like I'm currently ignoring the news report filtering through the living room and into the bathroom, where I decide to change my playlist from a soothing jazz one to current hits. Volume up, I begin humming to the beat while turning the hot water on to almost scalding just in case they decide to discuss Jason and the case against him. Because since his arrest, I've heard it all, and at this point, I'd rather ignore than confront the conflicting emotions simmering within.

What journalists have pieced together since his arrest hasn't changed much. Authorities aren't releasing more than where he met the woman still recovering, the ties to other murders, and *me*.

However, with each day that passes my ire builds. Fiery licks across my nervous system without provocation, and it's no one's fault but the monster still on the run.

I'm angry. Sad. Feel guilty because of my attraction to the man keeping me safe.

"Not now, Ava. You need this." Taking in a deep breath, I bring his masculine scent into my lungs and hold it there for a few seconds, letting it wash away my doubts. I need this reprieve from the torture because Elijah Ford is embedded into every inch of his home…

Sandalwood, mint, and a touch of sea salt.

It surrounds me. Haunts me. Invades my senses.

Branding my DNA with his mark, I've become addicted to this unique blend, looking for ways to fill my needs without openly seeking him out. Right now is a prime example of my weakness: I'm inside the hall bathroom doing something I shouldn't.

It's been a week since I caught Elijah unaware and napping on the couch—since he comforted me after a nightmare—and he's completely ignorant of my newly acquired creep-like tendencies.

One, I interact while not giving anything away and avoid all topics that cause me stress.

Two, I only admire him when he's unaware or busy.

Three, I find any excuse to escape if either point is tested.

Moreover, in those seven days, I've become a prisoner of my feelings and wants.

I'm insane for even contemplating anything past my survival at this moment; that's where my focus should be, and yet it isn't. Instead, it's on *him*.

And maybe it's because of the crazy, horror-filled ride I'm on that I cling to him, but stopping isn't an option. He's both a comfort and solace. Something I can hold onto, even if it is in secret and behind these four walls that I let go.

I need this release. It's the only way.

Stepping inside the large, walk-in shower, I stand beneath the waterfall feature and let the hot water soothe my aching limbs. I'm tense, my body strung tight, and I reach for the bottle of his shower gel he left in here two nights ago.

Why? I have no clue.

Am I grateful? Absolutely.

I pour a generous amount into my loofah and shiver. From excitement. From the fear of being caught. It smells just like him as I lather myself, rubbing his scent into my skin, while the man is downstairs working out in the on-premises gym.

Lifting weights. Running. Sweat running down his defined muscles…

I'm swallowing back the whimpers fighting to slip past my lips.

Elijah goes every day for forty minutes before breakfast unless he's working, and today, I broke down. So, while he thinks I'm sleeping, I'm taking advantage of his generosity. It's why I didn't change the news channel he left it on, choosing instead to indulge in the empty apartment and not risk him hearing me.

While he's sweating and flexing and being hotter than sin, I'm taking the edge off.

It also helps to know that I'm safe here. To know that Elijah has cameras pointing at the door—the only entrance to his home—so I can give in to my shame without an audience.

There's comfort in that, something I haven't felt in a while. I'm all alone and not panicking. Can enjoy this one minuscule selfish act.

I know that he's always close. Elijah has proven to me with mock drills that if the worst were to ever happen, he can reach me within minutes.

The iPhone in my hand buzzes with a text, the screen lighting up with Elijah's name.

Start the timer now. ~ Eli

K. ~ Ava

I'm standing by the front door, the timer counting down the seconds it takes him to get to me from the amenities floor of the building. Being so high up, we've already run the elevator route, but today, Elijah's taking the emergency stairs. The sparkly case in my favorite shade of purple makes me smile as much as it protects my new phone, both gifts from Elijah.

This is extra protection for the times he's not here. Eli's been called in to work a few times now, not for long shifts, but this way, if I need to reach him or the officers monitoring the building, I'd have a way to get help.

Because you can't run with a house phone, and I'm thankful for his thoughtfulness.

We also know this device isn't being tracked. No one has this number but him and his boss.

When the timer hits the three-minute mark, I begin to pace the foyer. Back and forth, I'm getting a bit anxious as we close in on the next sixty-second mark, but then he's there. Eli's pushing the door open and raising a brow before it times him at four minutes.

"How did I do?" He's breathing a little harder than normal, and there's some sweat, but nothing like I expected. If it'd been me, I'd be dying on the floor, heaving and moaning in exhaustion.

"Three minutes and fifty-six seconds."

"I can do better than that."

"I believe you, but how about a break? I'm a little thirsty." How couldn't I be? *His white T-shirt clings to every muscle—his pecs, and what is a clearly defined six-pack—making my mouth dry. Even his basketball shorts are sexy. The way they hang low on his hips show-casing his muscular thighs and calves...*

"What are we having?"

There's a small tinge of huskiness to Eli's voice and my face heats up; I quickly walk past him before he takes notice, calling his name over my shoulder. "You want water or iced tea?"

"You pick. I'll take whatever you give."

"He's making this so hard on me," I groan low, one hand on the shower wall as a shiver runs through me. The man is caring, patient, and dangerously handsome. He looks good in a suit and workout clothes, but beyond the physical, there's the fact that I trust him.

Crazy since I barely know him, yet it doesn't make it any less true.

It's scary and maybe idiotic, but my heart knows he's not here to hurt me. Elijah's a protector; he's a pure alpha male, which creates a different dilemma...

Every cell in my body is thrumming with need. To cum with a cry of his name on my lips.

This is so wrong. I should stop.

I know I'm pushing my luck, and getting caught is not an option.

There would be no going back. How do I explain this?

And yet, I don't stop.

Bringing both hands to my chest, I spread the suds across my sensitive skin which breaks out in goosebumps at the slightest touch. I shiver and bite my lip to fight back a moan while praying to God above that he gives me the will to stop.

Because while I've never physically been with a man, I do have needs. The desire to give in and find relief, to satisfy the urge that this man—Detective Ford—creates, is heady. Days on end of lust have made me weak.

I also don't have a vibrator here to help me. Just a tiny swipe of a pulsing toy would send me over the edge, a beautiful fall into an abyss I so desperately need.

"Elijah…" It leaves me on a whimper as I reach my bare mound and then lower, right over my throbbing clit and labia. I'm soft and wet, so slick as I slip a finger between my lips and part them while the heel of my palm presses against the trembling bundle of nerves. It feels good.

Sends a small pulse of pleasure down my spine and then spreads throughout my limbs.

Yet my ache intensifies. Grows with each touch.

I need more.

Pressing against my entrance, I push two fingers inside until the second knuckle and stop, savoring the way my body reacts. How tight I clamp down, and I can't help but imagine it's him. His cock, not my fingers.

How thick he would be.

How his hands would grip me and position me to his liking.

How I would let him.

My hips gyrate once, and then again. I want it deeper. To feel just a bit of the burn—how I would stretch around him—and I add a third finger.

At once, I tremble. I'm so close.

The heel of my palm adds pressure on each slow pump, and I can just feel my orgasm fast approaching when the door to the house slams closed.

"No," I cry out, fighting a different set of emotions. In the blink of an eye, I go from needing to come, to rushing out. The bathroom smells of his soap and my body is thrumming with a hunger I don't know if I can control. I need to get inside my room before I get caught or jump his bones, both high possibilities, and within seconds of the door closing, I have the water off and a towel around my body.

Not changing into the clean set of loungewear on the counter, I clutch the clothes to my chest as I contemplate the fastest way to my room. Where he'll go first, and how to not bump into the man.

Rational? No, but I'm a one-track mind with the destination of my room as the goal.

One foot in front of the other, I open the door and rush out without thinking, not seeing what is in front of me, and I slam into a wall of muscle.

A wall with strong hands that grab onto my hips to steady me. Whose fingers dig in, pulling a tiny whimper from me as I clutch my towel with my free hand to keep it in place. This wall smells like my kind of heaven and yet beckons me to become a sinner as our eyes meet.

Heavy-lidded, his hazel eyes smolder, and my breathing hitches. He licks his lips, and I bite the inside of my cheek while taking a step back. And then another.

Every processor in my body is blaring red and telling me to abort. To run.

To remember why we can't go there.

"Ava," Elijah says low, the timbre of his voice flowing over my skin like a caress, his large hands clenching at his sides. "Are you—"

"Bye!" I yell out, interrupting him. He's looking at me, and my body can't handle his nearness. The way his heat sears into my flesh. How good his hands felt gripping my hips.

Without a backward glance, I leave him just outside of the bathroom and rush into the room I'm occupying. I don't stop until I'm inside and the door is closed, cursing my stupidity and obvious reaction.

He's a temptation I can't avoid, and it could end in disaster for us.

We can't. Even if I want him.

Maybe I should ask for a different—

I stop that train of thought in its tracks. Feels wrong.

Because no matter how much I should, I won't. There's only him.

I want Elijah near me, even if it's just within the same building. Same home. Protecting me.

"How the hell do I make these desires go away?"

The truth is that the answer might just be scarier than the question.

chapter 12

CRIME SCENE - DO NOT CROSS   CRIME SCENE - DO NOT CROSS

DETECTIVE FORD

"Fuck," I hiss low, rubbing my eyes. A mixture of anger and exhaustion consumes me, and a headache is forming at the back of my skull, making it harder to concentrate. It's pounding, and all I want to do is rest, but I *can't*. Not until Jason Ripley is behind bars or dead from a bullet between the eyes, preferably from my gun.

I'm a man of my word, and I keep my promises.

Moreover, I haven't had a single good night's sleep since Ava arrived, and each encounter brands me. She holds a power over my being no one else has before. The sight of her in that towel a few days back almost annihilated my resolve, because job be damned, I want her.

Badly. Insanely.

Exhaling roughly, I stretch my neck from side to side and glance at the clock. I've been up for almost twenty-four hours now and should take a nap, but the information I'm currently dissecting won't let my mind settle.

Rest; something now foreign to me. Blue balls are also in my immediate future.

Get it together, Ford. You have a job to do.

Right. My job. The one I seem to not give three fucks about when I'm near her.

Refocusing on the laptop in front of me, my eyes feel the strain—everything on the screen becoming a bit blurry as I read through the latest information Captain Perez sent yesterday morning. The electronic file contains new details very few are privy to, and if the media got wind of its severity, we'd have a panic on our hands.

The sudden mass reports of bullshit sightings will pull us away from what could be a capture. I've seen it before: prank calls and false information flooding our offices, and manpower becoming thin as we work to confirm each one.

Scanning the picture in front of me, I take in the placement of certain items inside the shot. How his style of operation is changing, twisting, and the results left behind for investigators to find are careless. Sloppy, even.

As of the latest reports and findings, we have another body.

This is the second since Ava's been in my care and exactly fourteen days apart.

Another girl that looks so much like her, and it fucks with my head. My vow to capture this son of a bitch myself wavers for a moment as the urge to grab her and disappear forms around the edge of my subconscious. Not that I would, but the thought is tempting.

"We can't allow him the chance at another victim," I grit out from between clenched teeth. I'm pissed and it cuts deep to add another state to the already thick file: Texas, California, Arizona—and since she's been under witness protection—New Mexico.

Fifteen bodies now. Fifteen cases to sift through as I wait for the inevitable.

My mind won't shut down as I look through each crime scene photo, breaking down the similarities and jotting down the new habits.

His kills are becoming messy. There's a note of angry desperation in each gruesome scene.

Jason Ripley wants our attention. He thrives on her fear.

Clicking the mouse, I shift to the next set and come to a stop at the note found at the crime scene. It's tagged and numbered, the date stamp from three days ago. Then, there's the same block-like writing style brought on by the heavy use of an oversized-tipped Sharpie Marker. This is reminiscent of a homemade sign people make for games or concerts; it's meant to be generic, and yet there's the way he draws a line through her name and the letter "e" that's becoming a tell.

There's anger in that stroke. A lot of frustration.

It's also in the streaks of blood made using his fingertips beneath the two lines.

Possessive. Threatening.

You can't keep her from me.
Ava is MINE.

"I'll kill him before he lays a single finger on her head," I hiss out, making a note of the two drops of blood on the bottom right-hand side of the message. At the very edge, they're small, but we need to know whose DNA they belong to since they don't match the placement of the others.

At this point, I have to expect the worst.

Was this girl his only victim that night? Where is she from?

Closing the pictures, I open a PDF with vital information on the victim. I scan the document, looking for a picture copy of her ID, and stop short when I do.

> **From: Arlington, Texas (Approximately 25 minutes from Dallas)**
>
> *Sarah Wilson was last seen with her best friend, Karla Alvarez, walking toward the parking lot of a popular college bar in Dallas. Both attended the university there and were out with friends celebrating a birthday. Neither made it to their car, and security footage is blurry at best; yet, we have the description of a pickup truck that left minutes after the girls were seen stumbling out.*

I'm quick to pull up a missing person search for the area from two weeks ago to the present date, and it doesn't take long to find her. Everything here matches the details given to me in the email—going back and forth between the two, I cross-examine the information and realize that no one has connected this dot.

Their focus is on the deceased and not on the best friend. It's also not on the fact that they were kidnapped in Texas and her body found in New Mexico.

But where's Karla? Do we have a second body somewhere else?

"She might still be alive." *Christ*. Rubbing my temples, I go back to reading and, at the same time, collecting info for Captain Perez to disburse to those on the case. Thirty minutes in, and I have pictures, social media accounts for both, and the names of a few friends in attendance that night.

We need to find this woman before he...

My eyes scan the pictures from Karla's Facebook account again, and a few things stand out: her hair is bleach blonde with bright blue at the tips, and her eyes are brown. The colored strands are long and wavy, framing her face in a way similar to Ava's, yet not long enough. Her height is off, too. Standing beside the deceased in what looks to be a vacation picture, she is taller by a foot at least.

She doesn't fit his usual choice.

The sudden pitter-patter of feet across the hardwood floors pulls my attention, and I look up just in time to watch Ava walk across the doorway. She's wearing a white tank top and black yoga pants, while her feet are encased in a small pair of socks in the most obnoxious shade of pink. Awake and grumpy, she mutters something on her way to the kitchen, and I know it has to do with her need for coffee.

The woman is an addict, and I find it cute. In the two weeks since her arrival, I've found myself watching her when she's distracted. Cataloging little nuances—mannerisms that make her all the more adorable to me.

How her clothes must be folded before leaving the laundry room.

How she's drunk her weight in coffee every day with no issues or side effects.

How she hides from me because she's embarrassed by the kiss on my chin.

How she looks coming out of the shower with little drops of water sliding down her soft skin. It was my body wash that she used that day. My scent on her soft flesh.

How motherfucking hard it is to keep it professional when all I want to do is take her lips—make her moan for me as I wring every last drop of pleasure from her body. Make her see how good we could be together.

Keep letting her hide. My attention needs to be on this case and Jason.

Not on her. Not on those curves that are meant to be touched—adored and worshipped.

"Lord, help me resist this temptation. Amen," I say low, looking up toward my ceiling. From the other room, I hear her curse, and my cock twitches, thickening at just the sound of her voice. It's another sign that I'm *fucked.*

Pulling up the captain's contact info, I load up the doc with my findings into an email and hit send. Within seconds, my phone vibrates, and his name flashes across the screen with an incoming text message.

Reading it now. ~ C. Perez

Let me know your thoughts. He's on the move, and my guess is he'll make a pitstop in Arizona next. ~ Ford

Three tiny dots appear on the screen. Takes a few minutes for his message to come through.

Why? ~ C. Perez

Better question: Who is leading him back to Los Angeles? ~ Ford

Are you thinking there's a tail? ~ C. Perez

I take a second to answer him, trying to find the right words to explain my theory on Jason knowing we have Ava. I'm not trying to give away too much information as this is a conversation better had in person.

There are just too many coincidences, something I don't believe in. His escape was too easy, and the manhunt seems to be going slow. On purpose or not, neither add up.

Too close for comfort. ~ Ford

I'll be at your building tomorrow at eight a.m. sharp. Talk then. ~ C. Perez

See you in the morning. ~ Ford

Something occurs to me then, and I shoot him another message.

There's a file inside my desk that I need. Please bring it. The top drawer on the right. ~ Ford

Got it. ~ C. Perez

Tossing the small device on the table, I follow the scent of fresh coffee and bacon.

What I find upon entering my kitchen is utterly delicious and so fucking wrong. All thoughts stop, and nothing but this moment exists. No case. No worries.

Seeing her like this gives me a sense of domestication I never craved before. Of satisfaction. Being in a relationship hasn't been for me. Women like dating a man in uniform until reality sets in. This is not a costume for a late-night fuck session. My last girlfriend was years ago because she simply couldn't handle my job. The hours spent away, the sudden emergencies pulling me away from a movie date or late-night dinner, became too much for her.

I'm not the kind of asshole who doesn't understand the anger it might cause. I'd get pissed myself at times when called away, but just like I understood her job as a PA for the CEO of a production company—her long hours—I expected the same tolerance.

I'd never cheat. That's not the kind of man I am, but my job is important.

I'm honored to help a grieving family find any semblance of closure while at the same time, helping them find justice.

Yes, it could be dangerous, but I know what I signed up for. I'm careful, and over the years, opportunities to let off steam were very few and far between. Not a priority. The last time was more than six months ago, and up until Ava, I've been more than okay with that.

My life is my career. There hasn't been room for anything else, and yet, right now, I welcome this. Her. This yearning she brings out in me is fucking with my head.

I'm fighting the need to take her when protecting her must come first.

How easily I give in. Lose focus.

"She's fucking beautiful."

Ava is at the stove, oblivious to me as she hums, her hips moving from side to side. Cooking shouldn't be this attractive. Her total avoidance of my being shouldn't pull me in closer, but it does. I almost hate that I crave her.

She doesn't see me as I watch her flip a slice of bacon and then another. Nor when she cracks an egg and then whisks it for scrambled eggs because the woman doesn't like omelets. But that seems to be a recurrent behavior since arriving.

Since those sweet lips touched my skin. Since my fingertips dug into her hips.

Avoidance is her ammo, and it's driving me insane.

"Good morning," I say after another minute, having waited until she was by the sink to announce myself.

"Shit!" Ava gives a small jump and then whirls around to face me. Her blue eyes narrow, and her hips jut to the right as she places a hand there. Angry. A fiery and sexy kitten. "Do I need to put a bell on you?"

"Are you going to continue avoiding me?" I counter, and she looks away, a hint of pink sweeping across the apple of her cheeks. *Love how easily she blushes for me.* "Talk to me, Ava."

"I'm not avoiding per se..."

"So, what do you call hiding or exiting the room if I enter it?"

"*Not* avoiding?"

Crossing my arms over my chest, I raise a brow. "Are you asking me?"

You're playing a dangerous game, Ford. It's for the best if she doesn't get close.

"How about some breakfast instead of the early morning interrogation, Detective?" The hope in her voice, how vulnerable she looks, tugs at my heart, and I nod. Give in easily.

"Fair enough." Crossing the room, I walk past her, hand skimming her upper back as I make my way toward the expresso machine. Ignoring the small shiver that runs through her at my touch or how my fingertips tingle, I stop at the cupboard above the brewer and grab two mugs. I don't ask her how she likes it or make any other attempt at small talk.

I don't turn around and pull her close like I want to.

I don't tell her everything that's been eating at me for the past two weeks.

That I don't like the silent treatment. That I find her gorgeous.

How I wish we'd met under different circumstances. Normal ones. Ones where her life isn't in danger. Instead, I keep it simple and make us a double shot each, then take them back over to the sitting area on the other side of my island. In the fridge, there's some hazelnut creamer and half and half; I pull that out, too, along with the whole milk. All that's missing is the sugar, and I notice she's put the small container between our drinks while my back was to her.

I don't thank her for the gesture, and after a minute she huffs. *Cute.*

With a small smile on my face, I begin to make mine—all black with a splash of whole milk and half a spoonful of sweetener. I know she's watching me as I take the first sip. The second and third are the same, even more so when she plates my food and then places it in front of me.

She's hyper-aware of me, just like I am of her. Of this fucking pull that's making me act irrational. I'm not someone to get involved with or take a case personally, but this one is just that.

More than, because this son of bitch slipped through my fingers or the nature of each murder.

I think it's her. All because of her.

"Okay. I deserve that." Ava sits beside me. Setting her breakfast down, she reaches for the creamer and pours more than a healthy amount into her coffee. She uses the same spoon to stir hers, not asking if she can, and eyes me while doing so. Daring me to comment. "Truce?"

"What are you talking about?" I ask, swallowing hard when she brings the cup to her lips and sips, moaning a tiny bit at the sweet taste. My cock throbs—pushes against the cotton of my sweatpants, but I ignore the ache and focus on her. "You deserve what?"

"You were ignoring me."

"No, I wasn't." *Just letting you make the first move. Playing with fire.*

"Liar."

"*Per se*?" Grabbing a piece of bacon, I take a bite as I take in the apologetic expression on her face. So contrite.

"Touché," Ava says, her smile bashful while she smiles and holds a hand out. "Can we call it a truce and not bring it up again?"

"Only if you agree to watch a movie with me." I shake it, loving how small hers is in mine. How soft her skin feels. "I'll even let you pick."

"Even if it's a *super cliché* chick flick?" Her lips quirk up into a smirk before pulling her hand from mine and digging into her food. I let her eat for a bit, biting back my rebuttal until there's a single piece of bacon left on her plate.

"Hit me with your worst," I say then, a deep yawn escaping that I can't control.

Her brows furrow. "Have you slept?" She's looking at me with concern, and I like it. More than I should. "At all?"

"You're avoiding." With some egg on my fork, I pause mid-bite. "Or is that your way of saying I look like shit?"

"Jerk." There's a roll of her eyes, and she raises her hand as if to hit me, but pulls back at the last second. It's a bit awkward, and it's hard to hold in a chuckle when she lifts that same hand to her shoulder to scratch a made-up itch. "So, are you? Sleeping, that is."

"No. I haven't." I swallow my bite and grab my cup of coffee. Bringing it to my lips, I take a large sip. She's watching me. Wants an explanation, but I'm not telling her about the latest victim. Not yet. I'll deal with it tomorrow after speaking with Perez, once I have a better idea of just how out of hand everything is. "Now, which movie? I need something good to knock me out, and don't worry, you're safe inside my home."

"I believe you."

"Good. So, what are we watching?"

"Not telling." Her pitch is a bit high, and there's a brightness in her eyes I haven't seen before. A glimpse into the woman she is and not what he made her. "It's a surprise."

"Let me guess—"

"It's not going to be a sappy love fest."

"Really?" Because I'm not buying that.

"Why does that surprise you?" Ava arches a brow while a wayward curl slips from her messy bun.

"Because most women live for those dramatic encounters..." I shrug, pushing my plate forward "...it's programmed into your DNA."

"I should flick you for that comment," she deadpans, looking at me as if I were an idiot. "That, or I'll choose to believe you're super exhausted and delirious."

"I'll take that last one, por favor."

"Very well." Slipping from her seat, her hip lightly brushes my arm, and I bite back a groan. Ava's close and grabs my hand, and I let her, enjoying the way she all but drags me to the living room. Once there, I'm pushed onto the sofa. "Behave and don't move."

"Where are you going?" I call after her, but she doesn't answer. It takes a few minutes, and the longer I sit, the sleepier I get. Closing my eyes for just a second, I begin to rest a bit when Ava comes back. Opening one eye, I watch her walk over to my PlayStation and pop in the DVD, then pick up a remote and blanket from the loveseat on her way over.

She plops down beside me, leaving just enough space to be considered respectable, and then looks over. The heat coming from her body caresses my senses. Lulls me. "Yes?"

"What did you go get?"

"Season One of my favorite show on DVD. It's one of the few things I brought with me." Ava covers me with the blanket, only keeping a small bit to place over her thighs. *Fuck*, it smells just like her.

Sweet and decadent, and I inhale deep while letting it relax me. *Has she been cuddling with this one while reading at night?* "Which is?"

My voice sounds a bit far away. Between the warmth of the blanket, the plushness of the couch, and her sweet scent surrounding me, I find myself drifting.

"...Horror Stories." That's all I'm able to comprehend before sleep takes me under.

chapter 13

CRIME SCENE - DO NOT CROSS CRIME SCENE - DO NOT CROSS

DETECTIVE FORD

"What are we missing?" I mutter, looking down at the papers spread out in front of me. Every single inch of this wooden conference table is covered by one file or another, my private notes from when I was the lead detective on the case.

Pictures sit beside each empty folder; they're a diagram into the inner workings of Jason's mind, and even the smallest detail can be vital in capturing this motherfucker. *To save Ava.*

"I've been asking myself that very question since our texts yesterday," Perez says, studying the notes he was given this morning as an older couple walks by, and I look up to follow their movements into the elevator. We're downstairs, and the blinds are open inside the private conference space the building's concierge lets me use whenever I need it.

The window doesn't allow anyone to see in. Completely soundproof and debugged for listening devices, but more importantly, if anyone tries to sneak upstairs, they must walk by this room to do so.

It puts me at ease. That, and I have cameras. Plenty. Every-fucking-where.

So, while Ava sleeps, I work. Try to solve the pieces of this puzzle that's been plaguing me since I was given my assignment.

Jason has someone working with him. He has to have an accomplice.

Of that, I have no doubt, but who? And more importantly, from which department and state?

"And what have you come up with?"

"I hate to admit this, but your theory is correct, Ford." He sits back and chugs his coffee, the grimace on his face telling me it's gone cold and nasty. Or maybe it's the bitter pill of betrayal. "No one thought to look deeper, or those who did were paid to remain silent, but somehow—one of our fucking own is feeding him information. We know Jason *is* heading this way. The bastard got free, and instead of going south to Mexico and avoiding recapture, he's leaving a trail of victims that point straight back here. It's a fucked-up scene. He knows we have her, but it's a lead we can approach. We can intercept him."

I don't like it. Fucking loathe that they'll use Ava as bait, but it wouldn't be the first time this tactic has been used. Especially as the desperation to recapture him grows.

I'll protect her with my life. No one will harm her.

My reactions to her don't make sense and the sudden attraction is beyond my comprehension, but I don't doubt it either. Something about her calls to me. To my innermost caveman-like tendencies where the need to provide safety and care supersedes all else.

"And the other girl?" I ask, trying to remain calm. To not show just how far I'll go for her if need be. "Has she been found?"

As of late last night, they're looking into Karla and asking the public to come forward if she's seen. So far, the missing persons report has been spread from Texas to the West Coast.

Cap shakes his head, lips pursed. "No. Not a damn sign of her. Not so much as a bogus call."

"That's not his usual style, though." Rubbing my eyes, I sit back and take a sip from my own lukewarm coffee as I work through the chaos in my mind. I'm not seeing something, missing what could be a vital piece of information, and it's eating at me. "Her pictures are everywhere now, along with his mugshot. Why tempt fate and be seen?"

"What are you thinking?" His question forces my eyes back to the morbid shots on the table. *His* kills. "From the very first victim to the penultimate, they all follow a certain pattern. Upper body bruising, a deep gash across the chest, and his thumbprints embedded deep into their jugular. Each body lies face up and straight, with their hands intertwined over their abdomens and painted red with their own blood. That, and the cuts. It's almost like a painter with the strokes of a brush."

"All but—"

"The last," I finish for him. Picking up Sarah's photo, I point out that this kill seems rushed. Unsatisfactory for him. There's anger in the way she was just left behind with a broken neck.

"How many know about the contents of the email I sent you? Are we exchanging that information with San Antonio and Dallas?" Pushing my chair back, I stand and begin pacing the room. Scenarios play out in my mind, each one leading me back to his first kill. "What about the team here or Arizona?"

"It's a combined effort, but mainly the two Texas departments."

"Check relationships. Ripley had or has friends and a family. We need to figure out if any of them have a connection to someone on the force."

"You think they know Ava personally? Maybe from their childhood?"

"Everything is possible..." I trail off as my cell phone suddenly vibrates atop the table. My landline flashes across the screen, and I grab the device, pressing accept, but I'm too late.

"What's going—"

"Ava." That's all I give Captain Perez before taking off, my finger pressing the redial button when it vibrates again. "I'm almost there," I say, pulling the door to the stairway open; it bangs against the wall with a loud clang as I take each step two at a time. "Are you hurt? Someone at the door?"

The last is almost impossible with how I watched the entryways, and my app shows no movement there, but I can never rule anything out. As long as she doesn't open the door, she's safe.

"It's probably nothing..." there's a self-deprecating laugh that follows, and it carries a hint of panic "...but you said to tell you if anything creeped me out. I'm sorry if I'm bothering you while you work, but—"

"You can always call me. No matter the reason." Behind me, the sound of footsteps running up is loud and heavy but much slower. My head turns slightly, just enough to catch sight of Perez bounding up with arms full of files.

"Thank you." There's a pause and then a huff. As if she's annoyed with herself. "Someone called the house and he said my name, and it just felt…*off*. Didn't sit right."

"What did they say?" Opening the door to my floor, I rush through and run toward my apartment. "Name?"

"An Officer Denis Meyers." *The fuck.* My hand punches the nearest wall, and a chunk of plaster falls to the floor. I don't say anything, my mind whirling in different directions. Looking at every possibility. "Are you there?"

"Open the door." It leaves me on a harsh growl as I stop, hand on the casing. Ava squeaks on the other end but doesn't hang up, instead, she keeps me on the line while walking my way and then pausing on the other side.

I can feel her presence through the heavy wood.

Feel her eyes on my skin through the peephole.

"Look up, please." I do as she asks, and the turning of a lock follows. Ava opens the door to let me in and as our eyes meet, the tightness around her features softens. "You didn't have to rush back, Eli. It's just that I was under the impression that only you and Captain—"

"No one else knows, Ava."

"He's right," Captain says, a little out of breath from behind me. My hands clench at my sides, the effort to not pull her close and lock us away almost maddening. "Your location has been kept a secret from everyone in our precinct working this case. No one outside of myself and Detective Ford should have that phone number, much less know you're here."

My eyes are on hers as he speaks, taking in her body language—ready to step in if she's afraid of the unknown male moving past us and entering my home. Something I realize rather quickly is unnecessary.

I don't miss the way she gives him a small smile.

No cowering back. No distrust. Almost *familiar*.

They share a look I can't decipher, and then those baby blues settle back on mine. "Should we head inside, too?"

"Are you okay?" Without conscious thought, I reach out and take her hand in mine. Give those small fingers a gentle squeeze. "Need anything?"

"You're here now." Her voice is a gentle caress. So honest and sweet. And fuck me if those simple words don't make me feel a hundred feet tall. It also fortifies my need to keep her safe above all else.

She deserves to know how bad things are.

It's true, and I hate it.

Hate that the fears she's lost will be back.

Hate that once we step through my door things will get heavy, so I try to lighten the mood.

I give her a cocky grin and waggle my brows. "Is this your way of saying I'm your knight in shining armor?"

Her response is a roll of the eyes and a quick flick to my forehead. Hard, too. "Don't let it go to your head, but I do, and it's not easy for me to admit that either. Especially since I know you're keeping something from me."

The smile drops from my face. "Why do you say that?"

"Because I watch the news, Detective Ford." The hand encased by one of mine shifts seconds before her thumb runs over my knuckles. "I'm also not blaming you."

chapter 14

AVA

Elijah's hiding something from me.

Has been for the last few days. Since I got here, really.

It's this pesky little secret that comes to light every time he looks at me. That first glance always gives away his concern—the weight he carries on his shoulders is visible within those seconds before it's replaced with want so consuming that I drown in those hazel eyes.

A longing that mirrors my own.

Unexplained and so sudden, but it's also a reminder of why I can't give in to these desires.

The last thing I'd ever want is Elijah in danger because his focus isn't on what matters: finding Jason and making sure he never sees daylight again. For me. For past victims. Detective Ford can't afford to be distracted, and on the same note, I can't let my guard down.

"After you," Elijah says then, turning me to face the entryway before stepping back. Eli's fingers slip from mine and skim up my arm, then across my back to settle just above the waistline of my yoga pants. Low enough to tempt but still be appropriate. "I'll close and lock up."

With a brief smile, he gives me a gentle nudge forward, and a shiver rushes up my spine as his pinky extends to caress the bare skin there. "Thank you." It leaves me in a low whisper as goosebumps rise on my arms. Ignoring my attraction to him is getting harder and harder by the minute. Nearly impossible.

You can't, Ava. Don't put him in a position where he could be hurt.

That reminder—my motto—feels like being doused with ice-cold water. It centers me enough that I fake it the best way I know how and step away from his touch. Squaring my shoulders hurts, and so does the loss of that masculine scent of warmth and earth with a hint of sea salt that's uniquely him.

I don't stop until I'm in the living room, where another face greets me. "Hi."

"Good to see you again, Miss Perry." Captain Perez stands, hand extended toward me, and I take it, giving it a small shake before pulling back. Two steps are all I get before Eli is beside me and watching our encounter with curiosity.

"Likewise." There's an oversized chair to my right, and I take a seat there, ignoring the urge to move closer to the man currently driving me insane.

"*Again.*" Eli doesn't ask. It's more of a demand for answers.

"Yeah." My eyes flick to his boss, and he gives me a nod. *Okay. So, I guess this one is on me.* "We spoke through a video conference call when I was told I'd be transferring to Los Angeles. He was nice enough to try and give me some reassurance—explain what to expect and my accommodations." At my explanation, Elijah just stares. Nothing in his facial expression gives way to his thoughts. "He's the one that promised to place his best in charge of my protection. He gave me you."

"I see." That's all he says, and I look at Perez for some help.

Can I be mad at him? No. Not really.

Not when we *all* have secrets. Even if it's not done with malicious intent.

"How about we focus on what's important here." Perez's tone holds an edge of anger. It simmers beneath the surface, and once again, fear strikes me. I've seen the news coverage. The two missing girls. "What did Meyers say, Ava?"

"He wanted to know if I was alone. If Elijah left a file behind for him to pick—"

"Word for word, Ava." This comes from Detective Ford. His tone is brusque and full of ire. My eyes meet his, and gone is the soft look or cocky grin. At this moment, he's a no-nonsense officer of the law.

He's not the man who welcomed me into his home with a smile and calmed my fears.

He's not the Elijah who made a huge mess inside the kitchen, and I wanted to kiss stupid.

"Go on, Ava. Tell us what he said," Perez looks between us, sensing the tension rising.

"The phone rang twice, and I picked it up, thinking it was Detective Ford. All I said was *hello,* when the man cut me off. It happened so fast, and I felt off—he made me feel uncomfortable." Tucking my feet beneath me, I place my hands in my lap, nervously playing with an old silver ring that belonged to my mother. "He asked for you..." my eyes shift to Eli "...and when—"

Ford's eyes soften. "Exact words, sweetheart. Please."

Taking in a deep breath, I let it out slowly and give them a nod. "He said, and I quote: *'Where's Ford? Why are you answering his phone?'* I tried to respond, but he talked over me. He came across as agitated. *'Did he leave a file for me before leaving you alone, Ava?*"

"Did he mention anything about the contents of the file? Anything specific?" Perez asks. In his hand is a pen, and he's jotting something down atop a thick manila folder.

I shake my head. "No. Nothing about its contents."

"Did he say anything else?" This time, it's Elijah who speaks. He's sitting forward, clenched hands hanging between his parted, muscular thighs. His posture radiates a simmering ire. "Was there anyone else, male or female, speaking in the background?"

"No. Nothing. The man caught me off guard, and I asked him who he was and how he knew my name, but instead of answering, he just...*laughed.* His chuckle held an edge of frustration that gave me the creeps." Closing my eyes for a few seconds, I try to shake the memory away. I take myself out of that moment of panic and concentrate on my breathing. It takes a minute or two, and I'm thankful that neither man rushes me. When I'm ready—when my heart calms and I can speak without a knot lodging itself in my throat —I look at Elijah again. Focus only on him. "*I'm Detective Meyers, Miss Ava, and we'll be seeing you again very soon.* That's what he said."

Elijah stands abruptly, nearly tipping over the small coffee table in front of him. A candle and a small crystal vase fall, though, shattering upon impact. The small picture frame beside them didn't make out any better, either.

"I'm going to kill every one of those motherfuckers. Those sons of bitches are going to regret the day they were born—"

"Miss Perry, please give us a minute. He might need a moment or two to calm down," they both exclaim in unison, one in pure fury and the other with a decorum that's drowning within his own anger.

Exhaling slowly, I listen without hesitation and head to my room, but not before pausing at the hallway's entrance. I look at the detective from over my shoulder. "You owe me an explanation, Eli."

Not a request or plea. The man understands, and I won't elaborate.

Today. Tomorrow. In a few days.

It doesn't matter because I deserve to know just how much danger I'm in. Just how bad and out of hand things have become. Elijah doesn't look back at me from his place near the balcony doors; his head is hanging down, and his breathing is hard, but he does something that's enough for me.

He nods and whispers out a rough *I'm sorry.*

"Feeling better, Detective?" I ask the second he steps outside onto the balcony. It's been a few hours since his blowout reaction, the one drowned within his truth to avenge me and the lives lost at Jason's hands.

His anger was palpable. Still is. It took over and infiltrated every single inch of his home; a suffocating presence that made my heart clench, and not because he was any kind of threat. Not because I worry.

I want to eliminate anything that doesn't make him smile. Make him happy.

God help me.

When his boss asked me to leave, I felt a hint of relief, and I hated it. Hated that the small distance gave me a chance to think. To be strong enough not to give in to my desires of being his *more.* At first, I took comfort in my room, putting on noise-canceling headphones to drown out the explosive cursing—the slamming of something large against a wall—but nothing playing through the device came close to quelling my yearning.

This need simmers beneath the surface and is starting to control me.

Stop it, Ava. Elijah's under a lot of stress and doesn't need your hovering.

And I understand that. I also know that as human beings, we need to release pent-up emotions consuming us before we one day…*snap*.

He needs space, and I'll give it to him. I can't begrudge him, either.

Nor am I afraid.

Even if his anger was bad enough that Captain Perez took him out of the apartment.

Where did they go? I have no clue, but when the condo became too quiet, I left the safety of my room to investigate and found everyone missing, which led me to sitting outside on his balcony overlooking a bay that's too beautiful for words.

"Are you okay?" His voice is rough and hoarse, but beneath it all is a tinge of regret. "I'm sorry if I scared you, Ava. Please know that you're always—"

"I know." Turning my head to look at him, I give him a small smile. "Never doubted you."

"Thank you."

Standing, I walk to the railing he's leaning against and bump his arm. "Why are you thanking me?"

Elijah grimaces and then gives me a pathetic shrug. "I'm just glad you're not running from me. That you're not asking for a reassignment."

"Not happening, my dude." I bat my lashes while crooking a finger. Lightening the mood. "You're kind of stuck with me until this is all over."

"Is that so?" He chuckles, shaking his head before stepping fully into my space. There's less tension in him now, his smile a little crooked, and to be honest, it's very sexy. That swagger—his virile masculinity—causes my thighs to clench, and a tiny gasp gets caught in my throat when he looks up at me from under his thick lashes.

Not to mention how the side of his body warms mine. I'm surrounded by his scent.

Yup. I'm screwed. "It is."

"I'm very good with that."

"Good. Now, how about filling me in on..." I trail off because even though I hate to bring up something unpleasant, we have an overdue conversation pending. His truths. Mine, too. Especially after I saw that—

"Fair enough." He looks out onto the water. Neither of us speaks for a few minutes as we soak up the amazing view: waves crashing and a bright blue sky with a few high-rise buildings, each with a unique structural fascia making up the skyline. A rough exhale is my sign that he's ready. "Where do you want to start?"

"Adam and Jaime. That's when the secrets began."

"Would you like to take a walk with me?"

"Is it safe to do so?" I counter his question, liking the idea of going outside with him more than I should. My entire being vibrates with excitement at the opportunity to do something normal… *with him.*

Elijah nods again. "I'll take every precaution to ensure nothing happens."

"I know you will."

"That means a lot to me." Turning his face, his warm eyes settle on mine. "We've assigned two squad cars to be stationed nearby twenty-four hours a day until Ripley's caught. They're only a radio call away."

"Okay." Hopping a bit in place, I'm ready to head out. To not be cooped up. "And do you promise to be completely honest with me?"

"Yes." No hesitation. No doubt.

"Then yeah. I'd like that, Detective." *I just hope you grant me the same understanding in return.*

I'M SPEECHLESS. Horrified. Overwhelmed by everything Elijah's said.

My mind is going around in a hundred directions as I try to make sense of his words.

More girls. More lives have been taken, and each one is my fault.

Christ, will this nightmare ever end?

Closing my eyes, I try to fight back the tears pooling and threatening to spill—to not show just how helpless I truly feel—but I fail. A lone drop falls down my cheek, and Elijah wraps an arm around my shoulders, tucking me against his side.

"Whatever you are thinking...*stop*," he murmurs into my hair, placing the tiniest of kisses there. It's comforting, and if I'm being honest with myself, I want to burrow deeper into his warmth and never come out. "None of this is your fault, Ava. Do you hear me?"

"But—"

"None of it."

The vehemence in his tone pulls me from my temporary haven, and I look at him through watery eyes. My bottom lip is wobbly. "There's more to our past than what's in your notes, Elijah. I didn't know it was...I swear, I don't understand how I missed the signs when we were teens. How I didn't connect the dots now, but he…he—"

"Breathe for me. Nice and slow."

A hiccuping sob escapes, and it takes me another minute or two to calm down. To ask the question that's been plaguing me. At first, it didn't make sense. I truly didn't remember the name Jason Ripley, and there's a reason for that.

Not until today. That note.

"Why didn't Anthony or Rose tell me anything back then? So much happened, Eli."

"What are you remembering, sweetheart?" There's no reproach in his tone, nor does he pull away. Instead, his arm lowers to encircle my waist as he looks out over the water, letting me take my time. I'm in control.

"Everything began...*shit*!" The sound of a seagull suddenly flying close causes me to jump, my sharp yelp making the man beside me chuckle. We're sitting on a bench in an empty section of a pier not far from his building, watching a couple of small boats head further out to sea. A small moment of respite helps me gather my thoughts after those birds, and I'm ready to confess something only three other people know.

This isn't the first time that man tried to harm me.

Two more birds follow, and I duck a bit as one glides too close.

"They won't hurt you," Elijah says from beside me, but I can't turn away from them. There are so many. Most are perched along the tide pools below, yapping and cleaning their feathers before taking flight once more, some to feed, others to harass the people walking among them.

For the most part, they don't come near us, giving preference to a group of what looks to be tourists feeding them bread down below.

This scene seems so normal and is slightly amusing, considering the reasons we're here. The topic of our conversation. *What I need to share with him.*

It's also interrupted by the sudden loud ringing of Eli's phone. I shift my watery eyes over and take note of the way his jaw ticks, of the grim line of his lips. He's pissed yet remains cool at the same time while muttering a low *fuck.*

"Everything okay?" I ask, taking account of the sudden annoyance crossing his features.

"Yeah," is all he says before pulling the phone from his pocket, reading the message, and then returning it to its place. Those eyes of his are warm, though, as they meet mine, and the sudden apprehension that settled into my bones at once dissipates. "It's my mom, Ava. I owe her a call, and she's just nagging. I promise."

No rush. No anger.

I hold my finger up to him. "Pinky swear?"

"Pinky swear. No more secrets." Maybe it's childlike, but he follows through and links his finger with mine. A simple gesture, but it means everything to me at that moment—it takes a stressful situation and turns it into something that gifts me a semblance of comfort.

There's no urge to run, something that's a bit confusing yet true because I know in my heart that he won't abandon me.

This moment, full of heartache and fear, isn't hard to carry with him beside me. Someone who will listen. Help me. And maybe it's that feeling of ease, or the laughter of some innocent child down below that makes me talk.

"Something happened when I was sixteen."

chapter 15

AVA

"Ava, what are you—"

"Please let me speak, Detective."

"Sorry." Elijah turns to face me. No longer hugging me, his warm hand encases one of mine, and our fingers intertwine while his lips gift me a comforting smile. "But please know you can tell me anything without concern or fear of judgment. I've got you."

"Thank you." Reciprocating his grin, I reach for the bottle beside me. It's still cold, and I bring the ginger soda to my lips and take a few quick sips. Thinking. Mentally going back to another day and time that marked my life, a memory I once buried in the past due to my embarrassment. Stupidity. The fear of no one believing me. "Of course, back then, I wasn't allowed to see it as anything more than bullying or him being an ass, but *Lyle Janson Porter* tried to forcibly steal a kiss from me on my birthday."

Beside me, Elijah tenses; the muscles of his arm coil tight, yet his hold on my hand is tender. His stance is a bit protective, as if preparing himself for what's to come. This is also when he takes out his cell phone with his free hand, and Eli opens the recording app. He shows it to me. "Can I? This will remain private and used solely by me to help the investigation unless you give me your consent to share it with Captain Perez."

"Yes." He nods for me to continue after pressing the *record* button, and I sigh. Count to ten and then begin. "My best friend, Rose, and I were in my backyard that night. The birthday party was over, and it was just the two of us hanging out, gossiping like girls at that age do. You know?" I'm not looking for an answer; I just need a second to swallow and clear my throat. To blink back my tears. "I remember her giggles, the way she gushed about spending the night and possibly getting to see her crush from my bedroom window."

"Your neighbor being Salcedo?"

"Yes. Anthony."

"Go on, sweetheart." His tone is gentle, and I appreciate it. There's no judgment in his gaze, either. "All this will be very helpful."

"Okay." I lean forward and kiss his cheek. It's quick and a rash move, but I don't dwell on it. Instead, I sit back and close my eyes, letting the words flow before I chicken out. "Don't quote me on the exact time, but I'm guessing it was close to midnight when their 'crew' strolled through my backyard, reeking of weed and cheap beer. The boys were loud and obnoxious, and since we were supposed to be upstairs in my room, no one came looking for us. It was the norm, anyway. Everyone in our neighborhood knew they hung out on their side of the fence doing the same thing every Saturday night."

"So, no parental figures?"

I shake my head. "All asleep upstairs."

"How many of them came onto the property?"

"Three, but one had no interest and stayed by the entrance."

"Was this a fenced-in yard?"

"Yes." I tighten my hold on the bottle, and the plastic cracks under my grip—almost spilling some of my soda. "Our neighborhood was a relatively safe one, and it wasn't a high priority for my dad to lock the fence. Hell, most nights it stayed wide open, as did the families' across the street and even Anthony's." We were stupid. Too trusting. I've learned the hard way that security in itself is a fickle thing and can be taken at the snap of a finger. "And that night, they did just that, strolled on in and took a seat on either side of us. How did they know we were there? At the time, I had no clue. We weren't being loud, but you can imagine who I got stuck with."

"Jason Ripley."

"That's not his real name, Detective. Lyle Janson Porter is who I went to school with."

"Are you sure, Ava?" He's not being rude. Elijah's looking for a verbal verification because this changes things for him. For the investigation. "We have his legal paperwork and—"

"I might not have hung out with them like my best friend, Rose, but I'll never forget the names in that group. Especially the trio." It's why when the Texas DA asked about our ties as teenagers, nothing clicked. Even before and after the incident, I kept my distance from them. "What I said in my deposition about Anthony was true then; the guy was a nice athlete who everyone liked, and he loved manga—Rose was completely smitten by him—but that's all I knew. We said *hello* as neighbors, and his parents talked to mine, but it didn't go past that."

My best friend was possessive and jealous and I didn't want to lose her.

"And the others? You said they were a trio?" A group of men passes to the left of us, fishing poles in their hands, and Elijah tracks their movements. The expression on his face isn't friendly.

"Yes. Anthony, Lyle, and…Denis."

At the last name, his intense gaze swings to me. Jaw ticking. "Denis what?"

"I don't remember his last name," I admitted, regretting the fact I couldn't get my hands on the yearbook the district attorney needed. Maybe if I'd seen Jason's and Lyle's pictures side by side, I would've put two and two together sooner. "He was always in the background, getting high and following the other two. Anthony was the popular athlete, Lyle was a little more emo with touches of goth and dark hair, while Denis was quiet. He was always so quiet."

"You said Lyle had dark hair, but Jason's a natural redhead."

"He dyed it jet black back then." So dark and flat.

"How sure are you of this?"

"You can tell. Either in the regrowth between dye jobs or the staining around his hairline after."

"Is that why you didn't recognize him?"

"Among other things, and I'll explain after…"

"After what?"

"I tell you what happened after the three walked into my backyard."

"Before you continue, I have to ask. Did you tell them to leave?"

"No, and I've regretted that decision." For a few seconds, I look away. So much is going through my mind: my stupidity, the betrayal…shame. *No more hiding.* Meeting his gaze once again, I let him see all of me. *Please don't be disappointed.* "At first, it was weird but a tiny bit cool. You know? At that age, the thought of someone older—a senior paying attention to a sophomore—made you feel like you were the shit. I'm not going to say they were hot; Salcedo was the better-looking of the three, but they were cute enough and mature in our eyes. So I made a mistake and let my guard down, ignoring the signals that were blaring, letting an eighteen-year-old Lyle strike up a conversation with me. He asked questions and wished me a happy birthday, and in my young mind, I felt popular. Important."

"When did it get out of hand?" Eli asks, thumb rubbing across my knuckles. His grip on that hand hasn't eased. "Where was your friend?"

"About thirty minutes into the impromptu visit, they pulled out a joint and lit up. They tried to *puff puff pass*, but I said no while Rose went for it. You can imagine it didn't turn out so great for her when she coughed up a lung on her first hit, but hey, Anthony was rubbing her back, so she was on cloud nine."

"Then what? No one smelled the weed?"

"Not when it's a semi-windy night, and all windows are closed. To everyone, it's just *boys being boys* and listening to music at home while staying out of trouble."

"Trusting parents."

"Exactly," I say lowly, a little bit bitter at how different males are treated compared to women. "Then, after they tossed away the end, Anthony asked Rose if she wanted something to drink." I lick my dry lips and pull my hand from his as I grab my bottle to take another sip, trying to distract myself from the slight shaking of my limbs. "Of course, she jumped at the chance to walk next door. No matter how much I begged her with my eyes, she had blinders on and left me without thinking twice." My heart races, and my palms sweat. My breathing gets a tiny bit choppy. "It happened so fast. One second, I'm watching Rose walk past my gate, and the next, I'm on the paved ground with Lyle on top of me. I went to scream, and his hand covered my mouth, body pressing against mine." *My pretty little, Ava. We're perfect together.* "Beneath his hand, I yelled for him to get off, and just when I thought he would, the asshole brought his face closer, and I froze. His lips stopped just a hair's breadth from mine as his hand traveled lower, stopping a few inches from my chest. I remember my eyes watering and the feel of his breath on my skin. How the stench of cheap beer and weed made me nauseous. I was so scared and—"

"You don't have to continue, Ava. I can put it together, sweetheart," Elijah murmurs against my neck, and that's when I realize that I'm no longer on the bench but sitting astride his lap. I'm in his arms, held tight while he rocks us a little side to side, and I don't want to move. It hit me at that moment how much I needed this hug. For someone to believe me. "Just breathe in and out for me. That's it. Slowly."

"I'm okay." My voice sounds off to my own ears. A tiny bit panicky, and yet, the more my body follows the rise and fall of his chest against my arm, the tension drains. Breathing gets easier. "He didn't get to finish, Eli. Lyle moved to touch me, and I reacted, driving my knee as hard as I could into his balls. In agony, he rolled off, and I took the opportunity to run inside and lock the door."

"That's my girl." He goes rigid beneath me. I know he didn't mean to say that, and I'm not going to make a big deal out of it. Not now. Not when I shared something with him that's worn me down for years. Elijah clears his throat and mutters a low *Christ.* "And Rose?"

"Came back a few minutes later swooning over her first kiss." Elijah lets out a small groan as I shift in his lap, covering it with a cough. It's a horrible sound, and I almost laugh. I would even find it mortifyingly hilarious if I didn't feel so drained after my confession.

"She wasn't a good friend," he says, and the tinge of anger in his tone warms my heart. It shouldn't, but it does.

I lay my head on his shoulder, a heavy sigh leaving me. "Trust me, I know."

"How did you figure out who Jason is? Was it before today, and you were embarrassed or—"

"This is where I ask that you don't get mad at me…" His silence causes me to lift my head from the comfortable position. From where his scent is the strongest. Eli's giving me a pointed look, silently asking me to carry on, and I give a small shrug. Grimace a bit. "After you left the apartment, I walked into the living room and the files Captain Perez left behind were a bit messy, but what caught my attention was a note with bold black writing on it that had blood. I've seen that before."

"That note or?"

"Before the incident, Lyle invited me to a Valentine's dance that I declined. His flowers, a bunch of daisies, came with an oversized card attached and the same handwriting style. Bold, blocky, and with a possessive and pushy undercurrent that made me uncomfortable."

"I'm going to kill that motherfucker." Eli's voice is gravelly, almost a growl. The vehemence—his anger is palpable, but it doesn't scare me. Instead, I feel understood and vindicated as we sit in silence once again. Not that it lasts long. After a few minutes, Elijah nudges my shoulder. "Want to get out of here? Do something fun?"

That's one way to change the topic. "Is that your way of saying enough with the heavy?" It's my attempt at a joke, but neither of us laughs.

"It's my way of saying I need to see you smile again. That's all I want." Cupping my face in his warm hand, he pulls me a little closer and lays his forehead on mine. "How can I make you happy, Ava? How can I make it better?"

You already are. I almost say it. It's on the tip of my tongue, but I chicken out.

My face heats up, and my emotions are all over the place. From scared to angry to happy to starting to fall—

"Baking," I blurt out before completing that thought. A truth there's no coming back from. "I miss cooking and baking."

The hot water pelts down my back inside his shower. I'm sitting down on the floor, knees to my chest as I process the day. The tears have stopped, yet my emotions feel out of whack.

Everything we shared continues to replay in my head:

What he told me. What I confessed. What I still *haven't.*

How Lyle's attention always lingered: heated looks, trying to hold my hand, and punching my first boyfriend in the face for kissing my cheek after a school dance that same sophomore year. My parents and friends all thought that it was him seeing me as a little sister—being protective— because that's the bullshit line he fed them.

No one paid attention when I said I barely knew the guy.

That just because he was a close friend of my neighbor didn't mean he and I were close.

I didn't hang out much less talk to them. That was Rose, not me.

My solace came the day he moved away, but the cost for that reprieve has been too high.

I'll come for you.

For years, I lied to myself. I pushed him out of my mind and thanked God Lyle never tried to touch me again and took the rejection well, but the joke's on me. This nightmare will never end. Realizing that this is a lost cause is a punch to the gut, and another sob catches in my throat, causing me to bite down hard on my bottom lip so Elijah doesn't hear.

I'm screwed no matter which way I turn.

It's why I've been hiding since we came back to his apartment. Avoiding. Trying to make amends with a puzzle full of broken pieces that fit within its new perimeters. It's not supposed to.

I'm not supposed to think past surviving, and yet, I do. Want to.

With Elijah, I have hope. Have a chance at something uniquely normal, and it's scary because how can I think of wanting more when I don't know what tomorrow will bring?

Will they take me from here too?

Will Lyle or Jason get to me?

Will Elijah want anything to do with me after this?

And yet, despite all those lingering questions, there's a blooming force growing within that scares the bejeebers out of me. A woman running for her life shouldn't be focusing on her handler. I shouldn't like how good he smells or feels against me. How much and how often I think about what his kisses would be like, even if we've never moved past hugs.

Will I be alive to celebrate my birthday next month? A sobering thought.

My heart aches for all the families Lyle's destroyed. For the lives taken because I didn't speak up when I should have.

"Why did I ever listen to you, Rose?"

"Where the hell have you been?" I whisper harshly, wiping away a tear as I wait at the now-locked gate. The minute a hobbling Jason left, I ran out and closed it, standing watch and listening closely for any screams. I've sent her multiple text messages, called her phone, and was seconds away from yelling for my dad when she walked back over.

Alone and smiling. Blushing.

Chill. I'll be right over. ~ Rosie

That's all she sent me while I worried a hole in the grass. I didn't snitch on her, and it's all because of that single text. That, and the fact that I still don't know how to process what happened.

Maybe it's the shock. My anger and confusion.

The fear. Disgust.

"You're being a Debbie Downer when I've just had the best night of my life, chick."

"Are you kidding me right now? What you did was unsafe, Rose." My heart's still beating fast and my limbs are jittery—the area around my jaw is sore from Jason's hold. "What were you thinking?"

"That he's hot. That I like his attention." She giggles, touching the right side of her neck with the tips of her fingers. "Don't be mad, but I was busy enjoying myself. He's so amazing, Ava, and—"

"Jason forced himself on me," I blurt out, choking back a sob. A harsh shudder runs down my spine; I feel dirty. Can still smell him. "He knocked me down and climbed on top of me. Pressed himself while covering my mouth with his hand and...I couldn't scream."

"Are you sure?" She's still smiling, nudging my shoulder as if I'm joking with her. "It's probably a huge misunderstanding. A dick move, yes, but I'm sure Jason's just messing with you."

"He tried to—"

"No, he didn't." Rose grabs my hand then, her eyes pleading. "Don't ruin this for me, please. Besides, he's my future boyfriend's best friend, and no one will believe you."

"What the—"

"Ava?" Elijah calls out, tapping gently on the bathroom door. "Are you okay?"

"I'm almost out." Standing, my muscles protest from being in one position for a while. God knows how long, and as I rush to lather and rinse off using his shower gel, again, it hurts. My legs are half asleep, and I hold onto the small built-in alcove for balance. "Give me five minutes."

"Take your time. I'm actually going to—"

"Can't hear you! One sec," I yell out, slightly high-pitched. Turning the temperature knob to a cooler setting, I dip my face beneath the water to wash away the tears I've shed, hoping any redness calms down enough and I'm not questioned.

It takes a few minutes for me to regain full feeling and then turn the water off, grabbing a towel as I step out. Cool air hits my skin and I shiver, tightening the fluffy fabric around me.

He's still just outside of this door. Can hear the heavy steps of his boots on the wooden floors right before he stops and his phone rings. It starts and then stops, only to start all over again.

"Motherfuck," Eli spits out, and I have a feeling it has everything to do with whomever is calling. "Sweetheart, I need to—" he trails off as I open the door, stopping in front of him in a terry cloth robe. I'm not trying to tempt him, but there's no choice but to step out like this again when I left my clothing inside my room.

The same electrical currents flow between us—the palpable hunger and intensity from the last time we were in this position—yet we don't react. Instead, his body is tense and his jaw ticks, but those hazel eyes remain on mine. Ever the gentleman, and I appreciate it.

Now's not the time. *We can't be. I can't.*

No matter how much my body yearns for him to comfort me.

"You need to leave, and something happened."

Elijah swallows hard, giving me a small nod. "He's been spotted in Arizona."

"Go on. I'm fine."

"Don't lie to me, Ava."

"I will be when you find him." It's the best I can do, and his expression is one of understanding. Elijah takes a few steps in my direction, closing the gap between us. My skin prickles in the anticipation of his nearness. For a minute or two, the man looks at me with so much warmth that it creates butterflies in my stomach. Soothes my fragile soul.

It also makes my lips lift into a tiny smile no matter how much I try to fight it.

I lose myself in his stare.

"I'm going to give you your life back one surprise at a time." Bringing a hand to my face, he cups my chin and rubs his thumb across my warm cheek. "Please enjoy my kitchen while I'm gone."

That's all he says before walking away and out the door.

It's confusing. Leaves me breathless.

He's...*wait*. His kitchen?

chapter 16

AVA

As soon as I'm dressed, I rush out to the kitchen and upon entering, stop dead in my tracks.

Oh.

My.

GOD!

"Wow," I breathe out, in shock by what I'm seeing. Every single inch of counter space is full of items, the baking necessities needed to make some of my favorite creations. From pots and pans to sugar and flour—chocolate and fondant, and even a piping gun set.

They're new and good quality, making the excitement in me grow.

It's been so long, and giddiness I haven't felt in months blooms deep inside my chest with the rush of a freight train. It helps push away every negative thought, momentarily forcing back the living nightmare I'm currently navigating through into the back of my mind.

Ideas form as another reality takes center stage. *He saw me and listened.*

It slams into me, and I can't stop the giggle that escapes. This thoughtful act touches me in a way that leaves me breathless, and my heart beats rapidly inside my chest while my body feels as though I'm temporarily walking on sunshine.

Light. Carefree. Itching to start measuring my ingredients, but then I notice the small Post-It attached to a bag of semi-sweet dark chocolate.

When did he have the time? "Better yet, how long was I in that shower?" I ask the empty kitchen, my eyes pinging from one end to the other, cataloging the *melt-me-like-butter* sight in front of me. And for the first time in months, I'm not being drowned by my fear—I'm excited.

Every day and with each interaction, my desires for him grow. My feelings morph.

Before this is over, these flip-flopping emotions are going to give me a mental breakdown.

Doesn't this man realize that every smile or touch and the way he simply listens to me breaks down my walls and decimates the rationale that knows this is wrong? That we can't start something while he's my police-issued bodyguard? I can't afford to let my guard down, and neither can he, but then he does things like this and…

It's bad and oh-so-good but dangerous to my psyche.

It could be fatal for me. For Eli.

"I fell for him." Even as I say the words out loud, the truth behind them is undeniable. This screams romance-book fast, and it makes no sense, but I did. I walk to the island and pick up the note, reading the quick lines in his penmanship. They're simple and sweet, and that butterfly fluttering in my belly takes off at a rapid pace, causing my smile to go from small to cheesy.

Go nuts, sweetheart. Have fun.

AND most importantly, I like all things chocolate.

Yours, Eli

"He's freaking adorable," I whisper to myself and then turn on my heels toward his office. After my failure at avoidance and our truce, Elijah offered me the use of his laptop anytime I needed it.

Well, today I need it.

I have a Google folder full of recipes, and one in particular is calling my name. It's a chocolate and hazelnut torte with a hint of spiced rum that is to die for. My mother came up with this recipe when I was twelve, but over the years I've tweaked it—made it my own with an alcohol glaze each of the seven layers gets bathed in.

His personal laptop sits on his desk; however, I notice the files from earlier and his work computer are now gone. *Don't think about that. Don't ruin the moment.*

"Right. Get the recipe, and for the rest of the day pretend that everything is perfect. Enjoy his generosity and gift." Or as best I can. And I plan to, but my curiosity is also tingling, and instead, I take the opportunity to snoop a tiny bit.

See more of who Elijah is.

The room is a decent size and decorated with a warm sandy color on the wall and a white trim. A desk sits in the middle of the room with a wall of bookcases behind it, both in a dark and rich wood finish. On the left is a small table that holds what looks to be a signed basketball and a football helmet: teams from the state of California.

There's also a rug and a large picture of some sort of mechanical item that I can't identify.

Other than that, he has a lot of books:

On his shelf. The left side of his desk. Stacked high on the chair opposite his work area.

I love it.

My feet carry me to his bookcase, and I inspect the titles there, noticing that he owns a few of my favorite classics. There are also a few mystery and psychological thrillers. The one that catches my eye, though, is a very worn copy of the *Art of War*.

Taking it in my hands, I open to the first few pages and notice his notes within. From a favorite line to his interpretation, he's made it a mission to decipher each word in a way that aligns with his perspective.

It's endearing and as I read a few, I find myself smiling.

"Definitely too cute." Putting it back, I take notice of a picture on the next shelf. There's no denying the younger version of himself wearing a graduation cap from his high school, and the woman beside him has to be his mother. They look so much alike—black hair and hazel eyes with wide, infectious smiles. She looks so proud, and he's letting her have her moment.

He really is perfect.

I move on to another picture, and this one is from his academy graduation. Still a younger version, but more of a man—bulkier and with less of a baby face. Here, he has a well-defined jawline and kissable lips, strong arms, and sexy eyes.

You came here for a recipe, not to drool over his pictures.

"Right. Recipe." Taking a few steps back, I turn around and sit down in his chair. There's no password, so I'm inside and typing my email information within seconds. The very moment it opens, things change for me, and the happiness I've felt since walking into his kitchen evaporates. There are hundreds of unopened emails, all from the same address.

Each subject line is more desperate—angrier than the next as my eyes skim down the page.

"How the hell has he been able to do this?" Clicking on the arrow that takes me to the very last page, I look at the dates and realize that some of these go as far back as Lyle's time in custody. Multiple times a day. Every single day. "No. I'm not going to look at this anymore." Leaving the emails, I get up and rush out of the room. I'll wing the dessert. It's better for me that way. "I'm safe, and Elijah won't let anything happen to me."

I have to believe that, or I'll go insane.

"SOMEONE'S BEEN BUSY."

"Shit!" I yelp, dropping the plate I'm washing into the sink full of soapy water. It's so cold, splashing and soaking the front of my thin tank top. My hands hold onto the sink's edge, my heart racing as I try to calm the quick wave of panic. "Why do you keep doing that to me?"

"I've been calling your name since I walked into the house, sweetheart." He's not apologetic in the least. A little amused.

"Liar." But I also don't doubt him. I've done everything in my power to concentrate on our feast, losing myself in something that's always brought me comfort. When I'm in the kitchen, I'm whole. At peace.

"Look at me." And I do, my body turning around before I give it permission to. "Are you okay?"

"I'm..."

"The truth, please."

Instead of sharing how I'm feeling, I take in the items in his arms. How do you stay mad at a man holding a single sunflower and a bottle of wine?

The answer is you don't. So I pretend to be clueless because my resolve can only hold so strong, especially after the sweet surprise of allowing me to take over his kitchen. To bake.

God knows I'm already hanging onto a threadbare line of sanity and decorum. I want the items in his hands to be for me, but wanting something and it being a reality are two very different things.

Complicates my plans.

That I must fight this for both our sakes.

"Are you leaving again?" At my question, he shakes his head. This is bad. Very bad. "Someone gave you a gift, Detective?"

"I'm Eli to you, not Detective." Elijah's lips curl into a sexy grin as he steps closer. One foot and then the other, he doesn't stop until he's standing close enough that his masculine scent infiltrates my senses. That his heat sears an invisible tattoo of his name on my skin.

"What are you doing?" It leaves me on a shaky breath, goose-bumps rising across my flesh.

"Just giving you a gift." He reaches behind me and places the bottle of wine on the countertop, his arm brushing mine. My reaction is automatic; I shiver, and his eyes meet mine. Hazel on blue. "Is that okay? After today, you deserve to be spoiled a bit. Let me."

There's a plea there, and that's a first. The normally demanding detective is asking, not telling.

"Yes." A whisper. An agreement to give in, even though I know it'll be a mistake.

"Thank you." His hand lifts and caresses my cheek before stepping back, and it's with this slight separation that I become aware of the flower in my hand. The petals are soft and skimming across my skin. "Now, how about you explain all of this?"

I can't stop the blush that blooms and spreads, my lips parting as I try to come up with a good enough excuse and tell him what I've done. And, I've done a lot of *it*.

"How about you disclose when you bought all the bakeware and ingredients? When did you find the time?"

"The grocery store app and their delivery service."

"I was only in the shower for an hour and a half at the most." That might have come out on a higher pitch, my pointer finger doing a weird circle and then jab-him-in-the-chest thing. His pecs flex beneath my touch and my knees weaken for a moment. "It's impossible to have—"

"How about a thank you."

"How about you explain," I counter, an open palm now pressed to his chest.

"As I said…" His lips twitch, but Elijah's position in this ridiculous argument is strong. "I ordered everything while we stopped for ice cream on the way back from our walk. It was plenty of time, Ava. Just a slightly higher than normal fee for their troubles, and you had what brought this cheeky grin to your face."

Am I smiling? Yes.

Does the handsome devil have an answer for everything? Also, yes.

"Hungry?" I ask then, changing the subject.

"Are we hosting a party I wasn't aware of?" It's his turn to counter, and for a split second, his eyes lower, taking in the wet fabric clinging to my chest. I watch as he licks those lips, and when his hazel orbs meet mine again, they're heated. Hungry. Yearning. "And yes, I could eat."

Instantly, my thighs clench and my panties dampen. My body flushes with heat and desire.

God help me keep my hands to myself. Must not touch, kiss, or lick him.

"That's a bit dramatic, Elijah," I force out, and he just raises a brow as my blush deepens. "Fine. You said to have fun, and I went nuts. It's been a while since I've cooked—wanted to—and I made a few of my favorites. Besides..." I wave a hand toward the three desserts already cooling and then at his oven. "It's just a simple meal. A tiny way to thank you for everything you've done."

"You didn't have to do—"

"And you missed the part where I said, I *wanted* to."

"If you'll let me finish," he says, mock glare in place. "You'll know I'm thankful you did. I'm starving, and it smells amazing in here."

"Good." With that, I turn once more and open a cabinet nearby. "Do you have a vase?"

"Not a small one, but there might be something we can use." His deep timbre is an inch or two away from my ear, his front almost touching my back as he reaches overhead to pull out a tall drinking glass. Placing it beside my hand on the marble, he nudges it and then removes himself completely. "That should work."

"Yeah, it does." A bit shaky. Breathy. I busy myself by filling the glass and then placing the sunflower inside, making sure that it's leaning just right. "The food will be ready soon, and I hope you love enchiladas. I made them three ways like my mother did: green, red, and white sauce. Two with chicken and one beef."

"Love them. What do you need me to do?"

"Can you set the table?"

"Setting tables is my talent." When I throw him a quizzical look from over my shoulder, he just shrugs. "Something *my* mother made sure I knew how to do. It's my job at every family function." Eli grabs what he needs without another word and walks out toward the dining room, leaving me alone to collect myself, calm my breathing, and pull our dinner from the oven.

It's totally cute that his mother taught him that.

Not helping my situation...

He also gets brownie points for the flower.

I have to resist him.

"Hey, do you need help carrying that in here?" he calls out from the other room, and I almost bang my head on his cabinet. He's thoughtful, sweet, a bit cocky, and sexy in that unique way only a real man can pull off.

"No, I got it." Looking down at myself, I realize I'm still in a wet top and rush toward my room. That's what he does to me; I'm not paying a lick of attention, and that just won't do. I'm in and out in seconds. With a clean crop top on in a soft shade of grey, I stop at the hall bath to splash a bit of water on my face.

It couldn't have taken me more than five minutes tops, but when I re-enter the kitchen, the three small trays were gone. So are the sides of rice, beans, guacamole, and pico de gallo. I also hear the clang of a serving spoon as he scoops up a portion and I follow, entering his dining area and finding an intimate setting for two.

Our food is served, my glass is filled with wine, and his handsome face stands behind a chair pulled out for me to sit. God help me, it's too much. After everything he's done for me, the surprise and being so damn understanding, I give in.

All of me wants this.

I'm not strong, and before I talk myself out of it, I walk straight toward him and press my lips to his.

All. His. Fault.

chapter 17

AVA

Immediately, he stiffens, but I don't pull back. No, I stand firm, holding onto his shirt as I take a small nibble of his bottom lip. And it's that bite, that hint of pain, that snaps him out of his rigidness. Elijah Ford kisses me back, overtaking my senses as he growls low at the back of his throat, his tongue sliding against my lip, demanding entrance.

An entrance that I grant without hesitation.

This kiss is everything; it's passionate and bordering on desperation with just the right hint of sweetness I'll never find with anyone else. Elijah's kiss is possessive, fully overwhelming my senses as our tongues intertwine and explore. His large, strong hands cup the back of my neck, thumbs tilting my head to the angle he prefers. He controls this. Me.

Giving me what I need with his touch. Hard yet gentle. A delicious overtaking.

My tongue swipes the very tip of his, flicking it before pulling back to suck his top lip, and a hungry groan escapes him. It tumbles through me, settling on my clit, and I throb—squeezing my thighs tight as my panties become slick with my arousal.

I'm wet and tender. For him. All for him.

My nipples ache, and I can't stop myself from rubbing my chest against his. This time his animalistic sound is almost angry and I shiver, shifting closer, and there's no mistaking the hardness now digging into my abdomen.

How it pulses, flexing against the inside of his jeans the more we kiss.

My hands itch to touch him. To explore.

"Oh God," I whimper, and that small sound stops him. It's like a bucket of cold water being thrown over my head; the way he abruptly pulls his mouth from mine makes me feel like an idiot. Like I ruined everything. Elijah doesn't release his hold on my head, though, but instead stares down at me, making me feel self-conscious. "I'm so—"

"Don't." It's gravelly. So hungry. "I'm not."

"You're not?"

"Not even a little." His thumb rubs across my cheek once while his other hand takes one of mine, squeezing my fingers slightly. "But one thing at a time. How about dinner and some light get-to-know-you conversation before I kiss you again?"

"Again?" I raise a brow, and the tension in my shoulders drops. He's being playful; that's a good thing, and I follow his lead. "I made the first move."

"That's only because I let you."

"Are you kidding me?" My blue eyes narrow, my teeth aching to bite him again. Harder.

"What can I say? I'm irresistible." With that, he brings his lips to mine once more in a quick and soul-destroying kiss before pulling back. I'm a bit dazed after—smiling—but ready to smack him when he winks. "Now, feed me, woman. I want to cuddle with you on the couch and watch a movie afterward."

I'm so easy when it comes to him that holding myself back is nearly impossible after that first taste.

I'm truly and utterly screwed here.

WATCHING him enjoy the meal I made is sexual torture.

I'm sitting at the head of the table with Elijah to my right, a placement chosen for me while I was busy changing my shirt. I also couldn't argue with his nonsensical seating arrangement, especially with that devilish smirk and challenging gaze aimed at me.

The cook always has special privileges, sweetheart. Get used to it.

I was about to ask about those "privileges" when Eli shook his head and led me to my chair before taking his seat. He's so close. His scent enveloped me.

Which led me to my current predicament...

Watching this man enjoy the food I made is downright a sinful experience. Almost as panty-destroying as our earlier kisses.

Every compliment. Every moan.

Even the grunts between serving himself a second and third helping aren't conducive to good behavior on my part.

I want to climb onto his lap and taste that mouth again, especially as he lifts the bottle of imported beer and takes a deep pull. The way his throat bobs with each swallow makes my thighs clench, and I barely remain seated as he licks the stray drop of Dos Equis sitting at the corner of his lips.

It makes me want to lick him from root to tip. Taste him everywhere.

Behave. We can't. Must resist.

Exhaling slowly, I eat another forkful of my green enchilada. The bite is fiery, a tangy explosion with its smoky pepper sauce that clings to the soft, corn tortilla. The intense heat builds: a pleasant zing that melds perfectly with the seasoned, shredded chicken and the Oaxaca cheese.

Then, there's the refreshing crema. It compliments and cools my tingly lips, making for a dangerous combination.

I want more. I should be devouring my meal.

But I can't stop watching him.

Jesus, I am a mess for this man. Broke first.

Swallowing, I grin at him. Keep it as normal as possible. "Is it good?"

"That was motherfucking fantastic, sweetheart," Elijah groans, patting his sculpted abs after placing his fork down. "I'm going to need to up my workouts with you living here."

I'm trying hard not to read too much into that statement, but I can't help the butterflies fluttering in my stomach. Acknowledge how easy it would be to give in to my desires and...

"Favorite color?"

He says out of nowhere and I arch a brow, head tilting to the side. "What?"

"Come on, sweetheart, humor me here." His eyes crinkle a bit at the corners; he's amused. "This is a first-date protocol, and small talk is mandatory. I already told you this."

"You mean you don't appreciate my preference for quiet meals?" My mock indignation isn't fooling anyone. Neither are the goose-bumps rising on my arms as his declaration of this being a date sets in.

First date. Meaning there could be more:

Kisses. Touches. Eventually bending me over—

"We both know you were admiring the view." Cocky. A little flirtation.

"Was not." I lift my chin high while denying it. "But if you insist, we do this rapid-fire style."

"And we take turns."

"Sounds like a plan." My tone is still a bit snooty as I take a sip from my wine glass. The sweet notes from the Riesling pair perfectly with the richness of the sauces. A delicious balance. "And to answer your question, I'm a purple and black girly through and through."

"That's two colors, Ava," Elijah says, shaking his head. "Pick one."

"That, Detective, is a lie," I counter, narrowing my eyes. Lips in a pout. "If we treat it like an ombre, it's just one."

"That's cheating." He laughs, rolling his eyes at me. It's good to see him like this, relaxed and enjoying himself. Since I've been here, all he does is work, exercise, and then back to work. Rinse and repeat. Providing this brief break for the man who's vowed to protect me, filled his kitchen with everything I could need to bake, and appreciates said food...

No words. Just pure pleasure.

"You haven't answered." I tease.

"Blue."

It's my turn to roll my eyes. "That's such a guy answer."

"It's also the color of your eyes."

Fuck. Me.

I almost say it, too, but choose to behave instead. "Favorite go-to meal when feeling lazy?"

His stare is smoldering, almost as if he heard my earlier thought. There's a hint of a challenge there, too. "Peanut butter and jelly sandwiches."

"Bagel pizza." And yeah, I take another drink from my glass. Multiple little sips. "Right side of the bed or left?"

"Always the right," he answers quickly and leans closer, his knee brushing against mine. His scent wraps around me like a velvet stroke across my senses. "Unless you want to—"

"Left," I interject, cutting him off from whatever temptation he was going to throw my way. Pushing my plate away, I sit back and finish my wine. For a few minutes, neither of us says anything, yet the ever-present electrical pulse that flows between us sizzles.

There's no denying the wetness in my panties or the sensitivity of my skin, a heightened problem as my chest stretches the fabric of my small top. My nipples are throbbing stiff peaks, something my detective takes notice of right away. His Adam's apple bobs, and the hand around his beer bottle clenches.

That earlier kiss did nothing but solidify how easy this could be.

Our easy banter further proves that he's perfect for me.

Yet, it's the throb of my clit that has me blurting out, "One more before dessert?"

"Is it chocolate?"

"Obscenely so."

"Then hit me, so I can get my sugar on. Chocolate and your lips."

He's not making this easy on me.

"Cats or dogs?" I ask, ignoring his words. This is the only question that could be a deal-breaker for me. I'm an animal lover. I always wanted—

"Why pick when you can have one of each?" His answer crumbles the last of my walls, and without pause, I lean forward, slip my fingers into his hair, and tug his mouth down to mine. The kiss is passionate and raw—bites and strokes of the tongue—and the perfect ending to our meal.

Screw dessert. His drugging kisses are all I need.

I'll deal with the repercussions later. *Much later.*

chapter 18

CRIME SCENE - DO NOT CROSS CRIME SCENE - DO NOT CROSS

DETECTIVE FORD

My neck is stiff, but my left side is deliciously warm.

I'm sitting up on the couch, neck angled down a bit, and lending my shoulder to a companion who's driving me insane. More so after our meal. Those kisses. The feel of her small hand clutching my shirt—her hooded blue eyes looking at me with so much yearning—but as much as I want to devour her, I can't.

Not yet. Not after her confession yesterday.

After what that son of a bitch tried to do…

I've never wanted to kill another human being before, and brutally so. The many ways going through my head should be worrisome, each more gruesome than the last, but more importantly, they go against my badge. My oath.

Yet, for her, I'd risk it all. He's an animal.

I'm going to break his neck with my bare hands.

Her faith in me, the self-recrimination and pain over trusting the wrong people, made my already protective instincts go into overdrive. The feelings I've fought hard to ignore—my wants—sucker punch me in the face as I deal with the reality.

I want her. All of her.

Even if our current situation is dangerous and her security is my main priority, the feel of her lips on mine changed everything. *She kissed me. Twice.* Robbed me of my senses and then forced me to break quite a few protocols while I was at it.

I could lose my job because of those kisses, and I couldn't care less. Fuck it all.

Nothing matters outside of putting him down like the disgusting beast he is, so my girl can be free. Because Jason, Lyle, or whatever the fuck he decides to call himself next week is now more than just a case; he's my enemy.

He will pay for her tears with his blood.

Ava is mine, and I'm keeping her. She'll never be hurt again.

The sunlight filtering through the large, floor-to-ceiling windows is brighter today than normal, and I savor the moment. The peaceful sound of her light breathing and occasional hums. I like it. Love the way a certain brunette with soft lips murmurs my name in her sleep.

"Five more minutes, Eli. The gargoyles and unicorns can wait for their coffee." Her nose is now pressed against my throat, the small tufts of breath marking my skin while my cock swells to full mast. I'm hard as fuck while holding in my laugh, a difficult predicament.

Ava's an adorably cute vixen.

She's also warm and soft and delicate, my perfect fantasy within reach, and yet I do nothing more than enjoy this moment. Relive the memory of her lips on mine and how right she felt in my arms. How she let me dominate and hold her to my liking as I took my fill.

Because Ava Perry is something else.

A surprise of mixed signals, lingering looks, and that sweet flush of pink across her cheeks that makes me want to bite her. A '*we can't*' but '*I need you*' puzzle that I'm putting together one perfect piece at a time. But first, we need to talk. She needs to decide if this is something she's willing to try because after tasting that sinful mouth and swallowing her moans, I want it all.

The good. The bad. The dangerous.

No going back for me.

A small chuckle escapes me as the little thing tips her face in my direction, an unconscious act with full-on duck lips. An exaggerated pout. "We need to get up, sweet treat." That dangerous mouth quirks up at the term of endearment. "Come on. I'll start the coffee."

"No." Just like that and full of sass.

"I'll make strawberry French toast."

"No."

"Yes."

"Just thirty more minutes," she whines low, and I'm truly fucked with how adorable I find it. "Please?"

"You asked for 'five more' twenty minutes ago," I remind her, and she nips my jawline.

"I lied." Not an ounce of shame. Bratty. *Fuck, I'm in trouble.*

"You're already up." Even I can hear the amusement slip through my mock-stern facade.

"Too warm and comfortable. Just a little more, Eli." *Motherfuck*, my resolve breaks just like that, slipping deeper into the couch as I reposition us so she's comfortable and using me as a body pillow. Ava lets out a low sigh as I do and a few seconds later, a light snore follows. Hers or mine—no clue because I'm letting sleep take me once more, too.

THE NEXT TIME I wake up, I'm alone. A bit cold.

I'm also hard as fuck beneath the confines of my sweatpants. There's no mistaking the tent or my desire to be buried deep between her supple thighs. *Where the hell is she?*

The apartment's silent except for a low humming sound coming from the kitchen, and I find myself throwing my legs over the couch to investigate. I know this perpetrator, and *not* seeking her out is impossible for me.

The culprit is tiny and sexy; a dangerous breed of perfection that's turning my life on its axis.

However, the second I stand to my full height my body protests, aching from spending the night on the couch. *Next time we sleep in my bed.* Presumptuous, but I give no fucks.

I'm not going to fight what I know to be inevitable. Not anymore, consequences be dammed.

Throwing my hands up, I reach back to stretch and a few bones in my upper back crack, giving my neck a bit of relief. At the same time, my shirt rides up and as I arch fully back, thrusting my pelvis slightly forward, a tiny gasp makes me aware of her presence.

What those tiny sounds do to me.

I'm in no rush, though, and I turn my head toward the opposite wall where a large, ornate mirror hangs. She's there, lips slightly parted and eyes on mine through the reflective surface.

No running. Not hiding. For the first time, she's letting me fully see how I affect her.

"Good morning," I say and add in two more stretches to mess with her. "What time is it?"

"A little past eleven." It's a bit breathy, and as I turn to face her, my mouth waters at the sight of flushing cheeks, bright eyes, and her messy hair. "Lunch is ready. I-I was coming to wake you up and give you your phone. It's been going off nonstop for the last twenty minutes."

Immediately, I'm concerned but keep my expression neutral. After her confession yesterday and my suspicions about the "officer" involved in this case, I'm trusting no one. Going by what Captain

Perez said, her location was kept secret outside of a few people, and that didn't involve anyone else from my department.

"We need to move her now that her location's been compromised," I hiss out from between clenched teeth while Perez just looks at me. His expression isn't giving anything away while I pace the length of the conference room in my building. There's an eerie bout of clarity flowing through me. I'm composed and determined as the last few hours—our conversation at the pier—play in my head on repeat. Her tears gut me. Make me see red. She's been alone for years dealing with his sickness while the world ignored the signs. While those she trusted told her it was a lie. That no one would believe her. "My family has a vacation home in Colorado we can use. I'm sure she'll—"

"Ava stays here. Both of you do."

I pause with my cell in hand, and the resounding crack of my neck as I turn my head to look at him is loud. To his credit, the captain just holds a hand up but doesn't step back.

"I'm sorry, Ford, but my hands are tied here. They won't let me move her."

"What the fuck does that mean?" My tone is calm, but my ire is palpable. Walking over to the table, I place my phone atop the file there and turn to face him fully. "Explain."

"Watch the tone, Detective. I'm your boss and—"

"When it comes to her safety, I don't give a flying fuck who you are." Taking the remaining steps between us, I get in his face and meet his hard stare dead on. I'll quit right now and leave with her if I have to. "You're not putting her in danger to satisfy some DA's fetish of catching him with her as the bait. Not happening."

"I have no choice but to follow orders, Detective Ford." I can hear the remorse in his words. Take in how upset Perez is, and it's the only reason I keep my hands off him. It's why I don't storm out while sending the universe to go and fuck itself.

"I can't—"

"Then don't, Elijah. Remember what I said when I asked you to protect her?"

"At all costs."

"Exactly. And while I need to enforce the orders coming from above, I won't hold against you how they're interpreted. Do what you must. Whatever the fuck that is, but both of you stay."

"You're saying find a loophole."

"I'm saying I trust you."

"Is the coffee on?" I ask her, trying to evade any questions she might have, at least until after I find out who the call is from. Holding a hand out, I wait for my phone, but she shakes her head. "Give it."

"What's going on?"

"Don't know until I see who's calling."

Ava purses her lips while narrowing her eyes. "Swear?"

"Yes, babes. Give me a minute or two, and we'll talk."

"Fine." She rises to the tips of her toes and kisses my chin. Then nips my neck. Her small hand places the device in mine, and it begins to vibrate. "Go. I'll make you a plate while you answer. Deal?"

"Deal." My mouth lowers and I kiss her plump mouth, a quick, harsh kiss while my hand gives her ass a gentle smack. A taste. "I'll meet you in there."

"Okay." I don't miss how she pushes back against my hand. *She likes it.* I give one more love tap to her right asscheek before heading toward my bedroom, making a quick stop at the en-suite bath to brush my teeth and then wash my face. The phone vibrates again while I'm there, and I figure out who the culprit is.

"Hello, Mother," I say loud enough that my voice carries in Ava's direction while entering my office. The door remains open, and I pull the phone from my ear, hitting the speaker button so I can scroll through any missed calls. It confirms my suspicions; she's curious as to why I've been avoiding her. "Did someone die, or did the house burn down?"

"Don't get smart, kid." There's the sound of cutlery and then her sipping something. "Where are you? Are you working *his* case?"

There it is. She's worried.

"Yes and no." Walking around the desk, I sit and lean back, closing my eyes as the scent of fresh coffee infiltrates my senses. "I am working, but you know I can't share the particulars."

"Are you being safe?"

"Always." Knowing what's coming next, I lean forward and access my laptop to check my email. With the way things are—how no one's to be trusted—I made a new account last night that only Perez knows the address for.

"...the family business is suffering. You're killing me, Elijah."

"Not happening." It's a never-ending conversation between us. She wants me to run the publishing house our family owns, the one passed down by her grandfather, and it looks like my cousin will take over while I silently sit on the board. Not active, just as another shareholder. They love it and are passionate about discovering new authors, but it's not for me. My call has always been to serve and protect the citizens of this city. Saving lives is fulfilling—a challenge I thrive on. "But I do have something that might interest you..." I trail off on purpose.

Dangle gossip and she caves. She's lovingly nosy.

"Tell me." It's a demand, and I roll my eyes. Mom's where I get it from.

"I've met someone." She squeals so loud that I lower the volume on my phone. There's some gibberish coming from her between the excited noises women tend to make. "It's new, but—"

"I need to meet her and..."

I don't hear the rest as I focus on the screen. Ava's email was accessed recently, left open, and is displaying nothing but emails from him. Months' worth, and each more threatening than the last.

What the fuck? Why the hell didn't she tell me about these?

"...dinner on Sunday?"

"Mom, I have to go." A part of me feels bad for cutting her off, but I can't focus on anything other than what's in front of me. I'm angry. Disappointed because I thought we had established a mutual sense of trust.

"What's wrong, Elijah? What happened?"

"It's work-related." I'm clicking on the first email and reading through lines full of anger and desperation. Threatening. A psychotic love note. "I'll call you later. Love you."

"Okay. Please be safe."

I don't wait for her to hang up before I'm standing, tipping my chair back in the process. It creates a domino effect; the harsh push causes it to hit the edge of my shelves on its way down and a picture frame meets its demise. The crash is loud, but I could give a flying fuck.

The world around me could explode and shatter into a million pieces; I still wouldn't focus on anything but *her*. The words he sent *her*. On the slapping of *her* bare feet on my floor as she races toward this room.

Everything starts and ends with Ava Perry.

Don't force my hand, Sugar.
I will kill every last one of them, Ava, before I break you.
I'm going to propel you to the edge of fucking death, and then bring you back over and over again.

I love you.

"Christ, Elijah," she hisses out, hand clutching her chest. "What's going on? Why do you look like an angry bull ready to plow through a wall?"

"When were you going to tell me?" I know my tone is brusque and harsh, but her distrust hurts more than I ever thought it could. Feels like a betrayal after what's happened between us: the confession at the pier and then our kiss. *Because you love her.* Motherfuck,

I can't think about that. It's too soon, and I can't place a name on these emotions when only rationality should exist. "Explain."

"Wait a second." Ava holds both hands up while coming closer. She pauses on the other side of my desk, her expression pinched tight with concern. "I don't know what happened here, but don't take it out on me."

"Jason. Lyle. Whatever the fuck his name is," I spit out, flipping my laptop around for her to see, "has been contacting you, and I find out by accident? Why are you hiding this?"

"I was going to tell you, Detective." The use of my title cuts more than the lie. "To be completely honest with you..." At the raise of my brow, her blue eyes narrow. Dare me to challenge that statement, which I don't. Instead, I bite the inside of my cheek. "I haven't checked my email in months. Since the night before I found him—"

"Months?"

"Yes." My anger deflates at the sight of Ava's bottom lip trembling. I feel like the world's biggest asshole. "My phone and laptop...everything electronic I could use to check my accounts was confiscated to be monitored by the DA's office. I have no clue who has them or if I'll ever see those devices again, but more importantly, I wasn't hiding this from you or anyone. It scared me yesterday when I used your laptop to get—"

"Why check yesterday?" I ask quietly, carefully. I've done enough already and don't want her to be afraid of me.

"There's a folder in my Google account with cake recipes, and I wanted to surprise you." No sooner has the last word slipped past her lips that I'm around my desk and pulling her against me. She struggles a bit as her eyes become glassy, but I don't let go. Instead, I lift her off the floor, feet dangling with her chest against my own.

"I'm sorry." And I am. More than anything. "Please forgive me, sweet treat. My head's running in a million directions, and that's no excuse." Laying my forehead against hers, I breathe in Ava's small exhales. Take her decadent scent into my lungs. "Seeing his words angered me, but I should've never talked to you that way. It'll never happen again."

"Can I kick you if you do?"

"Would you like to do so now?" I'd take anything she did; I was an ass.

Ava shakes her head, lips still sad. "No."

Instead of talking to her, I jumped the gun. I'm anxious because this sick son of a bitch is still out there with a missing girl and getting help from those that wear a uniform like mine. Because the woman I love is in danger, and they are forcing us to sit here like sitting ducks.

There's no denying how I feel. How consumed I am by her.

I'm getting her out of here. Have to, no matter the cost.

Lifting her chin with the tips of my fingers, I give her lips a chaste kiss while wiping a lone tear with the pad of my thumb. "I'm going to make this right. I promise you." Another small peck and I pull back, releasing her from my hold, and once she's found her footing, I turn to leave. "My mom's house in Colorado will do until I can figure out our next stop—"

"Don't go." Ava's choked plea stops me cold, and I turn to face her, the crestfallen look on her face gutting me. "I forgive you. I know we're all under so much stress. Just…*please*."

"Ava, sweetheart." My tone is soft. Trying to be comforting. "I'm only going to make a phone—"

"I need you."

chapter 19

CRIME SCENE - DO NOT CROSS CRIME SCENE - DO NOT CROSS

DETECTIVE FORD

Her plea to not leave breaks me in two.

It makes me feel like a king one second and an asshole the next. I did that to her. Brought the worry from that first night back into her warm eyes when all I should be is the reason she smiles.

Why she feels alive again.

I can't fight this pull any longer. Fuck it, I'm done.

In two quick strides, I grab her hand and pull her tight against my chest. Ava trembles but never pulls away. Instead, she shimmies closer when a deep rumble climbs its way up my throat, and our eyes meet.

I see everything I'll ever need in her gaze. In the way those succulent lips part, a tiny gasp leaves her throat.

We're hungry. Longing. Need the other.

She's mine.

"Baby, I need you to use your words. I need you to be very clear with me."

"You. I just need *you.*" It's breathy and *oh-so*-sweet. "I want to be yours. I'm done fighting this pull between us."

My reply is just as honest. Without a single hesitation, I slant my lips over hers.

"*Fuck,*" I groan into her mouth, almost shaking as that pure decadence that is Ava slams into my processors. I'm gone, metaphorically lying at her feet as I take what will always be mine. From now until the end of time, I'm keeping her after I kill Lyle Janson Porter. I'll do everything and anything to convince her. "Are you sure? Because there's no going back after this."

"Yes." She pulls slightly away, looking up at me with so much tenderness. "I love you, Elijah. And while I know it's fast and crazy and the worst timing ever…it's the truth."

"I love you, too." My hands shake on her skin as I exhale roughly. "I've been yours since the moment I opened my door and saw you standing there. So pretty and needing me."

"I need you now." Her smile is blinding, a serenity I've never seen before crossing her features. She's relaxed and happy. How I always want her to be. Our lips meet once more, a renewed desperation taking hold of me. My fingertips dig into her flesh, holding her still as she tries to roll her hips—Ava's just as overtaken as I am, clinging to me.

She claws at my shirt, pulling it over my head and ripping the collar in the process.

To get closer. Skin on skin.

I'm all too happy to oblige.

My hands explore lower, gripping and squeezing until reaching her thighs; I take one in each hand and lift her. My girl smirks as I do, a shiver running through her while she wraps those sexy legs around my waist. Ava squeezes tight, her hands in my hair as our tongues caress—stroking—as I walk us in the direction of my room.

I'm almost delirious with hunger and stop midway, backing her against the wall to thrust a few times against her clothed core. Pleasure rolls through me as her heat grazes my cock, the engorged head throbbing with each bead of pre-come she pulls from me.

I want more. Every glorious fucking inch.

"Take me to bed, Eli." She's hot, and her thighs are shaking, lips parted on a needy whimper. "I feel safe with you. Need more."

Those words cause me to stop. My eyes close at the implication. "Sweetheart, are you a virgin?"

Because if she is...*motherfuck.*

Nothing changes, except for the fact I'll be her first and last. The only.

A thought that makes me want to beat my chest like a fucking animal.

"Yes and no."

"Explain, sweet treat," I grunt, rolling my hips while my teeth embed into her chin. The bite is meant to sting, but then I'm soothing the abused flesh with a few flicks of my tongue. "Have you ever had a man between these thighs? I don't want to hurt you."

"No. Never." Another keening sound. She's desperate to move, but the way I've pinned her against the wall leaves little to no room. "Just the use of a toy."

"Christ, Ava. You...*fuck*, baby." A heady haze of lust overtakes my senses then, the knowledge that this beautiful girl played with her pretty pussy back home my undoing. One minute we're in the hall, and the next, she's on my bed, bouncing twice before I crawl over her body.

For a quick second, I take her in just as she is.

Hair splayed across my white sheets, Ava's chest heaves rapidly and her cerulean eyes dilate. Her small tongue peaks out, swiping across her bottom lip before biting down on it. No words. So much fucking need reflecting back at me.

"Are you going to just...*oh*!" she squeals, a noise that quickly turns into a low moan as I rip her shirt straight down the center, exposing her perky breasts. They're encased in a delicate lace bra, a few shades darker than her skin tone. So sexy.

"You're perfect." This time, I'm the breathless one, barely holding onto my last shred of sanity.

"Come here." Ava beckons me with the crook of her finger. "Kiss me again."

"Where?" That blush I'm enamored with sweeps across her cheeks and down over the column of her throat, then lower. "Be specific, love."

"Let's start here," she says, pointing to her mouth. And I do as I'm told, happy to be her slave. My mouth takes hers, tasting her natural sweetness and swallowing her moans. She's soft in my arms, yet just as hungry—starving for my touch. Each whimper settles on the tip of my cock like an electric shock, and I'm pulsing—throbbing against the thick cotton of my joggers.

"Fuck, Ava," I groan, loving how she nips my bottom lip, taking the flesh between her teeth and sucking before traveling down to my chin. Then lower. She litters my skin with tiny bites, and I close my eyes, savoring the moment.

I want her to always be like this.

Wild and free. Beautiful in her agony. A desire only I can satiate.

"You feel so good," she whimpers low, her hips rising to meet mine. There are only a few pieces of clothing separating us, and yet her heat sears my skin, feeding the fire blazing between us. Her entire stay with me has been torture—a literal challenge—I was never going to win.

Since the moment our eyes met, I've been lost to her. It's my turn to return the favor.

Mark her. Savor her. Cement my ownership over her heart.

"Patience, sweet girl. Let me enjoy you." Embedding my hand in her hair, I force her to arch her neck while my other hand pins her hips to the bed. Her tongue yields to my kiss, matches my hunger, and intertwines with mine between small flicks. My body covers hers from head to toe; I feel each shiver as it runs through her, the way her nipples tighten into stiff, sensitive peaks beneath the thin lace.

"Please," she moans, spreading her thighs wider to accommodate my hips. My cock throbs as I press harder, pulling back just long enough to watch as I drag the jogger-covered thickness over her slick slit. The cotton shorts hide nothing from me; the evidence of her desire is clear to see on the wet patch at the seam of her cleft.

Another bead of pre-come slips from my swollen tip, rolling down the underside of my shaft while I reclaim her kiss, moaning into her mouth. "You're perfect, Ava. My perfect."

"Yours, Eli. I'm all yours."

"Tell me again. Say it."

"I love you."

"Fuck. I love you, too." I can't stop rubbing my thick length against her pussy. Once, twice, and a needy sound leaves her throat. I press harder, grunting as the pleasure escalates. Burning me. Consuming me.

Fuck, I need her. All of her.

She might not be a virgin, but she's never had a man between her thighs.

She's innocent. *Mine.*

Trailing my lips to her ear, I flick the lobe with the tip of my tongue. "I'm going to enjoy you, sweetheart. Every single inch of you. Slowly," I groan, trailing little nips down the side of her throat and marking her soft skin. "I'm going to savor you until you're a begging mess, and then I'll fuck you until my name is all you know."

"Please."

"Sweeter words have never been spoken." Slipping a hand beneath her, I undo her bra. Bare her to me.

"Eli," she gasps, arching her back in an offering. And I do, wrapping my lips around a perfect, rosy nipple before tugging on the sensitive tip. Immediately, she writhes and her hips lift, arching her back with every inch of skin I trace with my lips. How I cup a breast in each hand—weighing and squeezing the firm flesh. My teeth tug and pull on the tight little peaks, taking turns. Each bite borders on painful, something she likes, if the way she's moaning below me is any indication.

Ava, my girl, likes the pain. Enjoys the slight sting.

With one last flick, I traverse toward the dip of her stomach. The muscles quiver, anxious and wanting, while her scent swirls around me like a siren's song. I can't stop myself from skimming my nose across the waistband of her shorts. Can't help but lick a path from hip to hip as I pull the cotton down her thick hips.

They rise of their own accord, making it easier to take the offending clothing off before tossing it somewhere behind us.

"More. Everything." She's panting and beautiful and absolutely perfect. My eyes roam her body, lingering on the small wet patch of lace between her thighs before flicking back to those baby blues I love. "Please."

"Where do you want my next kiss?" My tone is rough, gravelly, and full of the all-consuming lust I'm drowning in. "Tell me." Ava brings a hand between us and lays her fingertips right over her mound. She's blushing, hand trembling but not holding back, and yet, I need more. "No, baby. Don't be shy. Be a good girl and use your words."

The moment I said *good girl* she clenched for me. Hard and multiple times.

She likes praise. That, I can most certainly do.

"Kiss my pussy and make me come," she whispers on a moan, eyes on mine. They're full of lust—heavy-lidded as she undulates against the hand I've placed over hers. The act pulls our joined hands lower, right over her trembling bundle of nerves. "Oh, God. That's...*more*."

"Are you going to be a greedy girl, too?" Together we rub her slowly through the lace, light little circles over her clit. Her wetness seeps through and onto my fingers, and I press my hard cock against the mattress to ease the pain. Not that it does much. My desire to slam in deep and fill her sweet pink pussy with my come is eradicating any semblance of propriety. "Answer me."

"Want you too much, Detective."

At her words, I push her hand aside and tap two fingers over her clit before possessively cupping her. "And you're driving me past the point of reason. I'm crazy for you."

"Then make me yours." Pretty little thing has no idea how wrapped around her finger I am. How I'll do anything for her. Settling between her thighs, I push them farther apart with my shoulders and inhale deeply. My nostrils flare, and my mouth waters; I can almost taste her in the air. See the wetness coating her skin.

"You already are." Turning my face, I scrape my teeth against her inner thigh and bite down just hard enough to leave a mark before tearing her panties off. The snap is loud inside the quiet room, the soaked fabric and her following moan taking a back seat to the sight of her beautiful little cunt mere inches from my lips.

She's smooth and wet and the loveliest shade of pink. Pure perfection, she's a gift from God himself.

"*Please*, make the ache stop."

I'm done. Have no self-control left.

I bury my face between her legs, eating her out like a crazed man. Licking. Nipping. Devouring every drop of her arousal as she cries out, body bowing off the bed as I fuck her with my tongue.

She should always be like this:

Lost in her pleasure.

Riding my face.

Coming on my tongue.

Ava's natural sweetness is an explosion to my senses, and I pull my pants off with one hand. My cock springs free, bouncing against my abdomen before I grip it tight with my fingers, pumping it in time with each lick. I twist my wrist on each downward stroke as she cries out my name.

From her entrance to her swollen bundle of nerves, I swipe the flat of my tongue up her core. More wetness. More cries for *more*.

"What do you want, Ava? Anything, and it's yours."

"Please." That's all she gets past the scream that catches in her throat as I suck on her clit—she shatters, breaking into a thousand beautiful pieces, but it's not enough. She's sweet in my mouth, and I haven't had my fill. *Never will.* Releasing my cock, I slide a finger inside her heat and pump in and out slowly. I keep her on that edge of hypersensitivity and so close, my lips on her clit not ceasing their torture. *Just a little more.*

Her pussy is slick, and the sound of her juices coating my finger on each entry causes my cock to dribble onto the mattress. My need is almost demonic. My desires are sinful.

But I won't stop until she's as gone as I am. Until she's crying out her need for me.

Her walls pulsate and tighten their hold on my finger. "Elijah, I can't...oh *fuck*!" The second I scrape my teeth down her bundle of nerves, she explodes. Harder than the first time, she tenses, and her hips lift off the bed. At the sight of her head thrown back and coming from my mouth, I crawl up her body and position the head of my cock at her entrance.

I rub back and forth, dipping a little inside her tiny hole and pulling out to draw out her pleasure. I do this a few times, waiting for those eyes to focus on mine before I slide into the hilt.

"Motherfuck," I groan, grinding my teeth while trying not to move. Breathing in and out does little to help. Not when the room smells like us. Not when she's so tight and wet. Her walls pulse and my cock gives a small jerk inside her. I'm losing the battle. Resisting my natural need to flip her over and mount—fuck her—is overwhelming.

"Elijah, I—"

"I know." Bringing my face down to hers, I peck her lips once. Twice. "Tell me when you're ready."

Being her first time, I'm giving her a few minutes to adjust. She might've played with toys in the past, but they couldn't have been big, as her hold on my cock is near choking. For her, I bite the inside of my cheek and pray for mercy. I wait until she smiles at me, and her pussy clenches a few times, giving me clear permission to move. "Can I?"

"Yes." Those baby blues look up at me with so much want and hunger. There's something else there, too. A coquettish glint that causes my heart to beat like a war drum, for my cock to pulsate in time with her intake of breath. "Claim me so I'll never forget I'm yours."

chapter 20

CRIME SCENE - DO NOT CROSS CRIME SCENE - DO NOT CROSS

DETECTIVE FORD

Those words are my undoing.

A taunt. A challenge which I gladly accept.

"I love you, sweetheart." Before anything, Ava needs to know that I'd die to protect her.

"I believe you." The teasing look softens. Her pussy clenches hard. "And I love you, too."

"Good." Trailing kisses across her cheek, I pause at her ear and flick the lobe. "Now, tell me who owns this pussy? Who owns you?"

"W-what…oh, Eli!" I slam back in and ride her hard. It's not gentle. Not the way I thought of taking her for the first time, but it's us. Crazy and all-consuming and full of this love that has overtaken our senses. Immediately her pussy clenches, trying to pull me in deeper as her walls grip me tightly—fluttering around my girth with each entry.

My balls contract. They're heavy and full; I'm going to fill every one of her holes with my seed. "Squeeze me just like that, Ava. Let me feel you," I grunt as another rush of wetness bathes my cock and then pools on the sheets below. I'm not being gentle or sweet, but she loves it. The nail marks scoring my back are the proof. "You're taking me so well."

"Eli, I'm... *fuck*!"

"That's it, sweet treat. So perfect." My eyes traverse her body, taking in the flush that sweeps down her chest, how hard her nipples are, and the beads of sweat that caress her skin. Then there's how her stomach muscles clench with each punishing stroke, how she writhes beneath me.

Pleasure overtakes her senses, and a guttural growl builds inside my chest as I watch her.

Feel how tightly she's stretched around me. More wetness. The sound of her desire is the soundtrack to our love. The slap of skin. How she soaks me in her juices, and those tiny cries set my blood on fire.

Her tiny cunt looks obscene stretched around my girth, so fucking beautiful, but more so is the way she squeezes me. Tight, wet, and *motherfucking* perfection. She was made for me.

Taking her hips in my hands, I lift her off the bed and onto my thighs. This angle is much deeper and leaves her completely at my mercy as I manipulate her movements, piston into her at a near-punishing pace. It's maddening how much tighter Ava is like this, and I won't last much longer.

"So close." Her eyes close, and her mouth drops open in a silent scream then as I shift her pelvis.

"Motherfucking come, sweetheart. Give me what's mine." Tightening my hold on her hips, I lift and slam her down my length, thrusting in and out, gritting my teeth as the pleasure becomes too much. "Look at me," I growl out, never ceasing my control.

How I manipulate her on and off.

Blue eyes open; they're heavy-lidded and unfocused. "*Please*."

That's all she says. She's too far gone into her pleasure.

I love it. Her like this.

"Are you my good girl?" I punctuate each word with a thrust, grinding her clit on my pelvis on each downward stroke. She barely nods, nails digging into my arm. They break the skin. Sting. "Answer me."

"Yes."

"Then come for me. Now." Slipping a hand between us, I rub her clit, three tight circles against the throbbing bundle of nerves, and a scream tears itself from her throat. The orgasm sweeps through her small body, taking her under a veil of bliss while my name becomes a mantra on those sinful lips. "Just like that, beautiful. Bathe me."

"Elijah." A sigh. A whimper. Every single one brings goosebumps to my skin.

I can't talk. I'm gone.

My cock grazes a spot inside of her then that makes her silken walls clench hard. It's a massage—a pulsing, near-painful wave that pulls the come right from my cock. It's sudden and harsh and motherfucking nirvana as I hold still and empty myself, filling her to the brim and then some.

All for her. Every single drop.

Rope after rope leaves me and mixes with her juices, making a heady mess. We soak the sheets, and the room smells of us; I position my body next to her tired one as the reality of what we've done hits.

Not that I would change a thing. My caving was inevitable.

Pulling her closer, I settle her head on my shoulder while nuzzling the crown of her head. She doesn't move or talk, and neither do I. Instead, we just are.

It's nice to lay with her like this. More than.

This is something I want to do for the rest of my life. *One day, she'll be my wife.*

A sobering thought, but it's not a lie. She will be.

"I'll always keep you safe, beautiful," I whisper low so as not to disturb her. And yet, as if she understood, her reply comes in the form of a tiny snore that brings a smile to my lips. It's cute. It also further cements another truth: Jason will die by my hands alone.

Fuck playing by the rules.

I'M PULLED from a deep slumber by the sound of moans. A low, keening sound is followed by the stroke of a soft hand on my hard cock. The hold is tight, and her skin is like silk. Then there's the feel of her hair sweeping over my thighs and a hot panting breath grazing the engorged head, a come-inducing sight that pulls a few drops of pre-come from the tip.

She's also bare: flawless skin and flushed cheeks.

I jerk in her hands, a sudden movement that causes her to gasp and flick her eyes to mine. Happy and hungry. So sexy. "Beautiful, what are you—"

"I'm curious." Blue orbs, heavy-lidded and aroused, look at me as her tiny pink tongue swipes over the slit. *Christ.* Pleasure, red hot and electrifying, travels down my body and settles on my aching balls. Sweeps down my length. It thickens between her pouty lips, settling on her tongue as she opens to take me inside.

Every cell in my body comes alive; I throb with each bob of her head. How she hums at the back of her throat, hollows her cheeks at the taste of my flesh on her tongue. Ava's small mouth can't take all of me, and I enjoy the obscenity—her determination to do just that. On her next downward stroke, I hit the back of her throat, and she gags, choking on me a bit as spit runs down my shaft.

Those eyes water, and I groan, fucking loving her need to please. To taste all of me.

However, when I come, it will always be inside her pussy. At least until this raging inferno of lust subsides.

Grabbing a fistful of hair, I pull her off, entranced by the single strand of saliva that connects her pouty lips to my dick. "Get up here."

"But, I was—"

"Now," I hiss out, my hold tight. "I need you to ride my cock."

Ava scrambles into position, hovering right over my length, and then pauses. "I've never done this before, Elijah." There's a hint of fear mixed with excitement in her tone. In the way, she looks deep into my eyes. "Please, teach me?"

Teach me. So trusting. So mine.

"All you need to do is what feels naturally right."

"You are my *right*." She gyrates slowly. Testing. Rubbing the bulbous tip from opening to clit. "Now, show me. Teach me how to make you feel good."

This woman. This marvelous and crazy woman. She has no idea how wrapped around her pinky I am, how she owns me so completely that I'm losing my mind.

"Everything is right as long as you're next to me."

"I love you, too."

A groan leaves me as Ava grips the base tight and holds me against her. "Just like that, sweetheart. Guide me inside slowly," I grit out through clenched teeth, fighting the urge to grab those hips and impale her. "Roll your pelvis a tiny bit and…*son of a bitch.*"

She drops her weight suddenly, and my back bows off the bed, thrusting upward and pushing in deeper. "Will it always feel like this?" Ava asks, almost breathless, while lifting halfway off and dropping down once more. Then again. She's taking my length in fast little movements, bouncing in my lap as sweat beads at her brow. And I watch, transfixed, as two drops roll down and between her breasts before they disappear at her navel.

Ava doesn't need guidance. She's perfect.

Naturally sexual and decadent. Coquettish while maintaining a purity that brings me to my proverbial knees. Her pussy feels like liquid sin, and her walls flutter around my girth, jerking me off at a torturous pace.

Watching her like this, head thrown back and doing what feels good, is sexy. But more so is how she guides my hands to her hips, silently begging me to take over.

To fuck her. To make her come.

"For the rest of our lives," I vow and squeeze, digging my fingers in as I guide her movements. Yesterday was fast and hard, while today will be loving. No matter how much she whines and tries to fight my hold, I keep us steady, building us higher with each roll of our hips.

Sitting up, I skim a hand up her spine before cupping the back of her neck. Her body's flush with mine, taking me in deeper with the change in angle. It's more intimate. Our breaths mingle, taking in the other's exhale while our lips hover and eyes connect.

"Eli," she cries out, wrapping her arms around my shoulders—gyrating over my cock—and I pull her down. Her clit rubs over my pelvis, and her wetness coats my heavy balls. "I'm so close. This. Us—"

"I know." Because I'm right there, too. Licking at my spine, pleasure thrums through my limbs as I pump in and out of her. "Come for me, beautiful. Let me feel you."

The last word hasn't fully passed through my lips when she does. Clenching. Arching her back. She kisses me, moaning into my mouth as I fall right behind her, coming deep inside and not pulling out. I'm tempting fate in a way that could be dangerous, but I just don't care.

She could get pregnant. We haven't used anything.

It doesn't scare me, though. Instead, I pull her impossibly closer. Hold her tighter so there's no space between us and make sure my cock keeps her full. Just the way it's meant to be.

"Why are you smiling?" she asks while grinning herself. Eyes soft.

"We didn't use a condom." No reason to hide it.

"We didn't." There's a hint of fear in her tone now, and she moves to get off me. That's not going to work.

"No."

"No?"

"Yes."

"Elijah, you're confusing me here. Why aren't you freaking out?"

"Because today, tomorrow—a year from now, Ava, it will happen. Sweetheart, I'm keeping you."

"I—" She's cut off by the ringing of my phone. First, my cell and then the landline, and we both share the same look. Both go silent and then a text comes in. "You should answer that."

Ava gets up then, wincing a bit.

"Let's get you in the shower first, and then I'll—"

It's my turn to be cut off with her finger on my lips. She leans over me, standing beside my dresser and holding my cell phone in her hand. Her look says it all. She's worried. "You can spoil me later. Deal?"

"Deal." With that, she leaves, throwing me a sexy smile over her shoulder before closing the door to my bathroom.

The phone in my hand buzzes again, pulling my attention away from her and toward the device. It's Perez, and his message changes the direction of my morning completely.

He's been spotted. Empty warehouse in Yuma
with the girl. ~ C. Perez

Come in, I'll send McGrady and Stein to watch the
building. Let's bring him in and end this. ~ C.
Perez

> We leave in thirty. Not up for discussion. Copy. ~
> C. Perez

I'm typing out a response before processing it all, another kind of energy taking over. This one is thirsty for vengeance.

For every life he took.

For Ava.

It's time to end this sick motherfucker.

chapter 21

AVA

I'm restless. Scared.

Full of worry. A gut feeling that's made me scrub Elijah's home from top to bottom—work myself into a state of exhaustion that keeps my mind from falling down the rabbit hole of despair. From thinking the worst.

That he's hurt. That he's in danger. That he's out there looking for Lyle, God knows where.

So many things could happen. Could go wrong. And what's worse, I can't do anything to stop this.

Keep it together. He'll be okay.

"Breathe in and out, Ava. Everyone will be okay," I repeat for what feels like the hundredth time. My mantra. Maybe if I say it enough, I will put it into existence. But then I remember another set of words.

Words he told me a few weeks ago.

He's human. We all are.

And it's that *what-if* that's killing me. It's hitting me so hard in the chest because I failed to stay away. I fell for him. Completely and utterly.

Moreover, while I didn't mean to, I'm paying the price of my stupidity.

Not that it could be stopped, but I knew from the moment our eyes met that being together would hurt. That letting my walls down would be my—our—downfall.

If he doesn't come back home in one piece, I'll—

No. I won't even entertain the idea. Can't.

Closing the top drawer of the dresser inside my room, I stretch my neck, and the small pop it gives doesn't ease a single bit of the tension there. Instead, it pulls a bit, and I hiss in discomfort, bringing a hand up to massage the sore spot while holding my clothing with the other.

I'm stressed and tired. Need him to come back home to me.

"Any minute now, Ava. Trust him to know what he's doing." Dropping my towel, I slip a pair of yellow polka dot boy shorts up my hips and then a pair of his boxers that I stole while washing his laundry. A tight tank top with a built-in bra in the same black as his underwear finishes my attire.

It's comfy. Makes me feel closer to him somehow to wear something of his.

With a quick spritz of body spray and my hair thrown up in a messy bun, I'm out the door and heading back to his kitchen. Well, almost—my favorite pair of socks, fuchsia and fuzzy, go on my feet first before heading to take out the trash.

There's a chute near the center of this floor, and I feel okay throwing it out by myself, knowing that Elijah went after Lyle. That while I hate him being anywhere near the asshole, Eli knows where

Lyle is, and that's not in this building.

Before opening the door, I look out through the peephole and see nothing. I stand there for a bit and watch, and after there's no movement for several minutes, I open the door.

For some reason, the moment I step through the threshold, my skin breaks out in goosebumps, and my breathing picks up. Foreboding takes hold, and I pause just a few steps away. There's something in the air all around me, something that makes me want to run back inside and lock myself away.

I'm being ridiculous. No one's here.

I know this. Can see this.

"Just take the garbage and get back inside. No one is here. You are safe." Nodding to myself, I take a second to inhale deeply, letting out each breath slowly to help calm my nerves. Five times I do this, and it's on the last one that I begin to feel a bit of ease seep through.

My heart loses its galloping beat; the harsh thumping slows as my shaking limbs cease to twitch. Freaking out while Elijah isn't here won't help me or this situation, and I repeat that thought along with my mantra enough that I'm able to follow through with the simple task of dumping the garbage.

Sure, I rush to do it, but I focus on the positive: that I did it.

It takes me longer to clear my head than to do the task, and within minutes, I'm back inside. The soft thud of the door closing is a welcomed noise, and more so is the click of the lock that follows. There are two of them that I turn before setting the alarm and walking toward his living room.

On the way there, I make a quick pit stop inside his kitchen and grab a can of Olipop. I haven't had dinner, and eating something right now isn't going to happen with my nerves being shot, so drinking something with a hint of sweetness is the next best thing.

And it's while I'm in the kitchen that the house phone rings.

My first thought is that it has to be Elijah, and I rush to grab the cordless device from its place inside his office. The room is dark, and I pause near the entrance. That's not how I left it.

Before taking a shower, I made sure that every room had one light on.

"What the fuck?" I whisper, my heart racing as I reach for the small switch on the wall to my left. Finding it isn't an issue, and within seconds, I flip it. Nothing happens, though, and I do it again. Off and on. Off and on. "Lightbulb must've gone out."

It's the only plausible explanation, and I step further inside to reach the still-ringing phone. I'm just a few steps away when it stops, only to start again within seconds.

Grabbing it off the corner of his desk, I hit the talk button. "Hello?"

"Ava." Elijah's voice comes through the line like a soothing balm. At once, my body calms, and my breathing begins to settle. Just hearing him—knowing he's okay—gives me back the calm he took with him when he walked out the door. "You okay, sweetheart?"

"I'm...I've—"

"Everything is okay." *Christ,* how I needed to hear those words. "I just wanted to let you know that I'll be back a bit later than anticipated, but it'll be tonight. Don't wait for me to eat."

"And you promise all is good?" Taking the phone with me, I walk out of the darkness and head straight for the couch in the living room. The early evening sky is gorgeous this time of day, and I sit, looking out as we talk. "There's no reason for me to worry?"

What I want to ask is if they have Jason. If my nightmare is over.

"None. I swear." Voices are coming closer, and then a few doors close, like that of a vehicle. My suspicions are confirmed when the engine of a loud car starts, and then a siren follows. "I'll call you as soon as we get back. Stay inside and wait for me," he yells out, and I nod as if he could see me. "Did you hear me?"

"Yes. I'll stay in. Just come back safe."

"I'll always come back." That's the last thing he says before the click, signaling the end of our call. His words reassure me, and I listen. Truly let them sink into my heart and mind as I grab the remote and turn the TV on, flipping through a few channels until I find one of my favorite shows playing on a marathon. Dr. Pol is the bomb, and I let his amazingness take me away and distract me with the cuteness of a state fair and the kids with their pets.

I make it through four episodes before my eyes become heavy. Each tick of the clock is a struggle to stay awake, and as the intro to another episode begins, I give in.

Sleep takes me, but it's restless. Uncomfortable.

I'm dreaming, floating through an abyss of nothing as a giant screen in front of me plays out a movie reel of that night. I can hear his laugh. His promise to come back for me.

No one will save you. You're mine, Ava. Always have been.

There's a sensation over my right arm. I can't quite make out what it is, but it feels wrong. Makes my stomach turn as the invisible grip tightens. It's painful, and I whimper out, tears running down my cheek as the helplessness settles in. Even in my dreams, I can't escape him.

Feels so real. Even his breath on my skin is the same—produces the same taste of bile in the back of my throat.

You'll pay for your betrayal, pet. Bathing in his blood will be your penance.

Images flip through my subconscious, each more grotesque than the last, and as one of a dead Elijah takes the forefront, I awake, sweaty, panting, aware that something isn't right.

Throwing my legs over the side of the couch, I begin to stand. "It's just a dream," I say, my voice low and shaky. My eyes shift over to the sliding glass doors, and I take in just how dark it is already. *I must've been asleep for a while.*

Still, there's an unsettling feeling that runs down my spine, and I shiver. And it's in my mild panic that I notice that the lights that were on are now off. Nothing except for the television remains on, and I need to remind myself all over again of Elijah's words.

"I'm safe here."

"Are you?" As the words slip past his lips, the small lamp beside him flips on, illuminating Lyle's rough features. He's angry. A bit dirty. He's also standing while holding a large blade in his hands that he flips between his fingers without a care, not paying a lick of attention to the blood coating his skin, which appears to have a dozen tiny cuts. "Who's going to protect you, Sugar? That pussy fucking detective?"

"How did...?" The words get stuck in my throat. Fear—fight or flight—sits heavy on my chest, and I take a step to the side. Then another. I'm thinking. Begging God silently for a way out.

All I need is a chance.

"You shouldn't wander the halls alone, little Ava. Not even to throw away the garbage," he drawled, eyes hungrily wandering over my exposed skin. "Never know who's lurking."

"That's a lie. The corridor was—"

"My naive little girl." He tsks, thumbs running across the steel edge of the knife. "So lost in your emotions that you never looked toward the small alcove on your left. Not even a flicker of awareness as you blindly gave yourself an adorable yet useless pep talk before putting the garbage inside the chute."

"Christ." Another step, and he mimics me with one forward. "You've been here this entire time? The lights—"

"Me. I've enjoyed watching you again after all this time."

"Again?" I ask, just as his head turns toward the balcony and the night sky. Either he doesn't care or is extremely sure of himself because he doesn't so much as move a muscle as I rush toward the room's entrance.

"Are you looking to play a game?" That question makes me pause as I place my foot in the hallway, mind working quickly. "Perhaps hide-and-seek?"

"Answer the question, Lyle." I see my room door is closed, and so is the office, and curse my idiocy. *Head for Elijah's room. His closet has a gun and emergency phone.* It's a somewhat safe room; the door is heavy, thick, and in reinforced steel, as is the surrounding structure. Elijah told me bullets wouldn't get through and that if the worst came to be, to make it inside and hide near the far back so I'd be out of the line of fire.

It should hold him back long enough for me to call for help.

All I need to do is make it to the other side before...

"You first." Two large hands wrap around my waist, and I freeze. They pull me against an un-showered body, and there's no mistaking his hard cock as it presses against my ass. There's a second or two of shock and disgust and so much sudden adrenaline that I begin to shake uncontrollably.

My vision becomes hazy, and all I see around me is that woman inside his house. Her body. Her eyes as they lock with mine.

Blood. Red. It's everywhere.

A loud wail rends the air then, and it's full of this haunting terror that hurts my head.

"Just like that, little Ava. Scream for me." His breath is hot against my neck, and it's enough to silence the scream. To silence me. "Awww, baby. Don't stop. I rather enjoy you like this."

"Please." It's all I manage to get past the lump in my throat. "Why are you doing this, Lyle?"

"Took you long enough," he spits out, grip on me tightening to the point it hurts. So much so that I yelp, which makes him chuckle. "How could you forget me? After everything we've been through?"

"Let me go." It's a hiss through clenched teeth.

"You have better manners than that. Your mother was a stickler for it."

"Please."

"Was that so hard?" I don't respond, and he doesn't release me, either. Instead, he sniffs my hair—rubs himself against me—and it takes everything in me not to gag. To not further set him off. "You know, I changed everything about me for you, and it still wasn't enough. My hair. My clothes…"

"I never asked anything of you, Lyle, other than to be left alone."

"Fuck that, Sugar. If anyone's angry here, it's me. Don't give me any of that sass." He rubs himself against me, the knife in his hand stopping just below my breast. "I've been patient and more than kind, but you've never seen me. I tried it the nice way, and now I'm done waiting."

Keep calm. Get to Elijah's room.

Keep calm. Get to Elijah's room.

Keep calm. Get to Elijah's room.

Taking in a deep breath, I exhale slowly and toe off my fuzzy socks with the back of my foot, trying not to draw too much attention. He's busy burying his nose in my hair and muttering something too low for me to hear, but once they're off, I brace my feet.

"Leave, and don't come back."

"When I go, it'll be with you." Lips come down on my cheek, his tongue following the path down to my jaw, licking the few tears that have escaped. There's a deep groan that comes from the back of his throat a second before his hands tighten again—fingers painfully digging into my hips. "After I kill the cock-sucking pig that thought to touch what's mine, that is."

"What are you—"

"You think I didn't have eyes on you? The way he held you on that pier is—"

"Stay away from him."

"Make me." Those words awaken something in me. There's a sudden shift that I can't even begin to comprehend, and I don't attempt to. Instead, I let instincts take over, and I throw my head back with all my might. Screw the pain; I will fight back. Just the thought—his threatening words against Eli—seems to spark a sense of awareness inside of me that helps me push through the sudden pain of my skull connecting with his jaw. "Fuck!" he yells out, and his hold lessens just enough for me to use the momentum and stomp on his foot.

Once. Twice. Hard. With all my weight. My goal is to break his toe if possible.

"No, asshole. Fuck you!" I throw my elbow back, landing somewhere between his neck and face. It does the job, and I'm pushed away, a natural reaction from him, and I run. Take off toward Elijah's bedroom at full speed, and I almost make it inside when I'm grabbed once again.

This time, it's by my hair. Lyle pulls hard enough to force a scream from my throat, a sound that makes him laugh as I'm roughly turned around and shoved against the closed bedroom door.

My only escape is so close.

"Since when do you have a fighting spirit, Sugar? It's cute." His body crowds mine. His face tips down toward me. "Answer the question." I don't say a word, just bite down hard on my bottom lip to hold in my whimpers—to not give him what he wants. My pain. My misery. My fear. "I'll make you motherfucking talk, Ava. Don't push me this soon."

Another warning I ignore. His hold on my hair tightens, and I can taste the blood from how hard I embed my teeth. For some reason, his anger toward me turns into a sinister laugh a second later. His hold doesn't ease, but his eyes close, and his body moves back an inch or two.

Just enough space.

Just enough of an opening for me to bring my knee up.

This hit is different. Hurts him where all men are sensitive.

He drops before me like dead weight, almost bringing me down with him, and when he doesn't release my hair, I reach out with my hand and punch him straight between his legs. His scream makes me smile, and it's also the opening I need.

Two inhales later, and I'm inside Elijah's bedroom, slamming the door closed and turning the lock. For a few seconds, there's no noise. No movement. Yet, I don't wait for the inevitable.

Eli's closet is just across the room, and I dart toward it without conscious thought. The door is heavy, and it's hard to push closed, but I manage right before Jason crashes through the bedroom one.

It splinters, and debris flies everywhere, but I'm already safely inside. I walk the short way toward the back, where Elijah keeps a burner phone and Glock for me, and have the drawer halfway open when the first hit to the entrance comes.

It's loud, and I scream, almost dropping the phone in my hand. With shaky fingers, I tighten my grip and then hit the power button on the side. A low chime comes from the device before Lyle delivers another blow. "Open the fucking door, Ava. Don't force me to hurt you."

I don't reply. My focus is on the device in my hands.

On pressing the number *1* and bringing it to my ear.

It rings. Once. Twice. And then heavy breathing follows...

"Baby?" A bullet hits the door, then another, and I fight back the scream that wants to break through. My body's shaking, and I feel as though this is our goodbye. "Ava, what's happening? I'm on my way back...it was all a—"

"He's here, Eli. He found me."

chapter 22

CRIME SCENE - DO NOT CROSS CRIME SCENE - DO NOT CROSS

DETECTIVE FORD

Earlier Today...

I hate to leave her like this so soon after making her mine.

However, it's not something that can be pushed back.

Not when it's right within my reach to end this. Him. Everything.

Walking out of the building, I catch sight of a patrol car with two officers inside and make my way toward them. They're rookies; two guys I've seen in passing and don't give two flying fucks about. However, the woman upstairs, she's everything to me.

More so than my job. More so than my life.

The one behind the wheel sees me coming and taps the other on the shoulder. Both sets of eyes are on me. Sizing me up. *Fucking idiots.* Once I'm close, they roll their windows down. "Is there something we can do for you, Detec—"

"Anything happens to her, and it's me you'll have to worry about."

The cop on the passenger side bristles, his body tensing. "Is that a threat?"

"No." Both relax and even let out a small chuckle. "It's a motherfucking promise."

The laughter ceases, and it's the driver, Officer McGrady, who addresses me, his eyes narrowing. "Captain Perez will hear about—"

"I'll tell him myself. Word for word," I snap, slamming my hand on the top of the car. Eyeing the squad car's number, I catalog them for later tracking. I'm friends with many in my precinct, and having this one monitored won't be hard. "All that matters is that she's safe. No one goes in. Understood?"

"Understood," Stein says, holding a hand up in a show of peace. "We know how important this is, Ford. Everyone's on edge with the possibility of catching the son of a bitch."

"Then we won't have any problems." I give them a nod. "Just keep her safe."

WE'VE BEEN DRIVING for a little over two and a half hours now, and our destination is close. Adrenaline should be pumping through my system, my body thrumming with energy, and so far, I have nothing.

No bouncing of my leg.

No clenching of hands.

No itch to run out of the car and snap his neck.

From our report, we're so close to the asshole, and yet, ever since leaving my building, something's felt off. I have doubts. Lyle's in Yuma, Arizona, spotted and identified with a woman who's physically similar to Karla, but my gut says they're wrong.

To go back.

Yet, if there's the smallest possibility to catch him and save her, I can't walk away. To serve and protect was my oath, and she—they *both* deserve that I see this through. We have to get to her before—

"Everything all right with Ava?" Perez asks from beside me as he turns our headlights off and pulls into a desolate parking lot. The area has poor lighting and a few abandoned warehouses attached; it once belonged to an old mattress company that manufactured and distributed on-site.

Hell, even the old company trucks are still here.

"She's fine."

"Why the secrecy?" Instead of answering him this time, I open my door and exit the car, as do the officers in the other three squad cars with us: two from Arizona and one from Los Angeles. They want this scumbag off the streets. He's been watching me closely since we met up at his office. Gauging my mood. "Ford, if something's wrong—"

"I just called her to check in." I don't look at him as I walk to the back, pop the trunk, and put my bulletproof vest on. After we catch the jerk-off, I'll tell him and accept whatever disciplinary action the department gives, but not before. I'm not being pulled from this case. "She's worried, but okay."

"That's all?"

"That's all that matters." From our viewpoint, I see a few windows and an open door near the right side. There's a light coming from within; it's bright, and if I pay close enough attention, I can hear music. Old school rap. *What the fuck?* "Something is off, sir."

"We have to make sure." I can hear the doubt in his tone, but I still agree that we should. The captain looks at those with us, his face serious. "You all have your orders. Get in and save the girl. Keep her safe, but him, dead or alive, makes no difference to me. This ends here."

Everyone nods, and the men fall into line behind me while Perez stays outside with another member of our team. Their job is to watch the door and shoot, if necessary, anyone who runs from the building not wearing a blue uniform.

I give the command to follow as I walk across the lot, watching where we step to not alert them of our arrival. The closer we get, the louder the music becomes, and I hear two voices, both male, laughing about something.

Holding a finger up, I point toward the right, and two officers rush to the other side of the building, blocking any exit attempt. Once in place, I take my position and, on the count of three, barge in, guns drawn.

"Police! Down on the ground!" I yell out as the men behind me follow suit. There's a woman's scream from somewhere in the back and then the sound of shots being fired, then more, as a body crashes through a door.

My instincts kick in, and a red haze overtakes my senses. I'm on autopilot as I press the trigger—firing twice into the chest of a man raising his gun at me. He falls to the ground with a bullet hole in his neck, choking on his own blood as the life drains from his open eyes.

He's unfamiliar to me, but the man just behind him isn't.

Anthony Salcedo. Ava's childhood neighbor. Her best friend's ex-boyfriend.

There's anger in Salcedo's eyes as they meet mine, and he fires a shot, nearly hitting me in the arm. The bullet grazes my skin with no entry wound, and it lodges itself into a wall behind me. There are voices, loud and angry, yelling for him to drop his weapon, but he doesn't move.

His attention is solely on me, the barrel of his gun pointed at my chest. "You killed my brother, hijo de puta *(son of a bitch)*. I'm going to make sure you never see her again."

"Where is he?" That adrenaline I've been missing hits me with the full force of a battering ram, and I stretch my neck to the side. I need answers. He won't walk out of here alive, we both know that, but before he dies, he'll give me what I want.

"You're a fucking idiot, Ford."

"Answer me, cocksucker," I seethe. "Where is he!"

"Home is where the heart is," is all he says before firing another shot; it hits my vest-covered chest and throws me back, but not before I answer with one of my own. This one reciprocates where his landed on mine, except there's no vest to stop it.

Blood pours from the wound, and he falls, the gun slipping from his fingertips. It lands and goes off, but no one is hurt. Instead, it breaks a window of what looks to be a small office. Another female screams. Another victim?

My ears are ringing, and I shake my head to dispel it—trying to make sure that what I think is a scream isn't the aftereffect of being shot at. It doesn't take me long to figure out that it's not, and without thought, I stand on wobbling legs, rushing toward what could be a possible second victim. Disoriented, I kick the door open with my Glock in hand.

The room is small, smells of weed, and hides someone that I never expected to meet.

"Rose Marshall?" *Christ, this is going to hurt Ava.* The woman looks terrified, but not because she's been hurt. No. This one has some explaining to do. The way she's dressed, the loud music coming from an expensive Bose speaker, and the high-as-a-kite look in her glassy eyes tell me this woman was here of her own free will.

She helped them.

"How do you know my name?" Her voice is shaky, her body slightly trembling as she moves her arm to reach for something at her waist. A gun.

"Touch that, and I will be forced to shoot," I hiss out, already raising my weapon at her. "Don't force my hand, Rose. Use your head here."

"Where's Officer Salcedo and Meyers?" *And there is my connection.* "I'm his girlfriend, and this is—"

"You're under arrest for the aiding and abetting of a fugitive. For being an accomplice in the murder of—"

"Where the fuck is my boyfriend?" she spits out, frantic, as her eyes dart past me where there's another commotion. Sirens are getting closer, and from the way I see an officer carrying a small body in his arms from the corner of my eye, I breathe out in relief. Karla was here, and we've got her. "You can't do this to us. Ava needs this."

I can't stop my glare or the curl of my lip over my teeth. If looks could kill, she'd be dead.

But before she can try to fight me or reach for that gun at her waist, I'm on her, her hands behind her back, my grip tight as I cuff her. "You have the right to remain silent. Anything you say can and will be used against you in a court of law. You have the right to an attorney. If you—"

"Jason loves her and will make everything right between us." Tears run down her face now, leaving tracks of mascara in their wake. "She's my best friend. We all miss her."

Delusional bitch thinks they care about her and Ava? She's just another pawn in this game to them.

I almost pity her. Almost.

Gritting my teeth, I continue to read her rights. "If you cannot afford an attorney, one will be provided for you. Do you understand the rights I have just read to you? With these rights in mind, do you wish to speak to me?"

"Please," she whispers low, the reality of just how fucked she is beginning to sink in. "Where's my Anthony?"

There's not a single ounce of remorse in me as I stare into her eyes and say the one word that will break her heart. Not when they didn't care about Ava or her mental state. Not when they terrorized and killed so many innocent women.

"Dead."

"ANYTHING NEW?" I ask Baez, the officer who's been interrogating a still-wailing Rose—off and on for about an hour now—since we've been back in Los Angeles. She's inconsolable and wants my head. Been screaming obscenities that no one pays a lick of mind to.

What we want is answers. To stop Lyle before he reaches Ava.

Then, there's also my desire to get back to her. It's an almost uncontrollable need. A compulsion that's driving me insane as we wait. As I follow orders.

My job requests that I stay, but my loyalty has shifted and is with Ava.

Moreover, until Rose speaks up, Perez has me here. Waiting. Helping to put together a map to pinpoint Lyle's exact location. He's been warned, too. I'll give him another twenty minutes, and then I'm out. Fuck them all.

"Just that we're pricks and murderers."

I shake my head, picking up my bottle of water to take a sip. "What about Meyers?"

"MIA for two days now." At least we have a connection. Know where to start. "We have a squad car on the way to his home. They're picking up the wife and kids. That'll draw him out."

I'm not so sure, but don't voice it. Instead, I look back down at my notes and the latest information uncovered. The connection between Meyers and Salcedo.

Childhood friends who were on the force a few years back in Dallas, and partners at that. How Salcedo took the fall for Meyers during a sting operation focused on crooked officers taking bribes from a Mexican Cartel near the border trafficking through their city. One was terminated and served some time, while the other asked for a transfer here.

The trio kept in contact over the years.

Meyers flew under the radar and kept to himself. Blending in. Not calling attention to himself while being a good cop—and Salcedo waited. Planned. He bought properties in Mexico and Guatemala, with the final destination being Nicaragua.

He cashed in his favor to be a step ahead of every department. They had a network of officers accepting money and drugs taken from the department's evidence room after being logged in. That's how Lyle escaped and evaded recapture. Meyers was his eyes and ears.

Moreover, we had no reason to suspect Meyers until he called my home, and Salcedo wasn't in Los Angeles. And yet, I still feel as though I'm missing something...

"Have Stein and McGrady been made aware of the situation?"

Baez nods. "Yes."

"Has Karla woken up in the hospital?" Perez asks from behind me, placing his cup on the desk I've been using. "Did she hear anything that might be useful?"

"Unfortunately, no. She's still out and pretty banged up. Rose did a number on her, sir."

"Christ," I say, my disgust evident. "What's the prognosis?"

"Karla will recover. None of her injuries are life-threatening."

"And Rose?" I rub a tired hand down my face.

"She admitted to her part in all of this." Baez pulls out his recorder and hits play, letting us hear her for ourselves: how she used a baseball bat on her, how she found her cries of pain amusing. How she pushed the end of her lit joint into Karla's skin, laughing as the flesh sizzled and scarred. "Her lawyer is with her now, and we think they'll try to plead insanity. That she, too, is a victim."

I'll be fucked if that happens.

Karma is a bitch, and she'll get hers by the judge's hand or those on the inside.

As that thought crosses my mind, another one hits. Louder. Blaring across all processors, and I could just fucking shoot myself for not picking up on it earlier.

Anthony told me. All but laughed about it in my face.

Home is where the heart is.

"Motherfuck," I hiss out, rushing past everyone and toward the parking lot. Perez and Baez are behind me, yelling my name, but I can't stop. Not when I've been so fucking stupid. When I put her life in danger.

"What the fuck, Ford? Where are you going?" Perez yells from behind me as I click the fob in my hand and the lights of my Camaro turn on near the station's entrance. "Stop."

I'm inside my car before they reach me, the engine running before lowering my window. "He's here in Los Angeles. We need to go!"

"We don't know for sure. Don't know where he could be—"

My phone rings, interrupting him. At once, dread fills me, and my chest becomes tight as I pull out my cell and hit accept. "Baby?" I breathe out, not giving a fuck who hears. Nothing but Ava matters. What sounds like a shot being fired confirms my worst nightmare even before she speaks. "Ava, what's happening? I'm on my way back...it was all a—"

"He's here, Eli. He found me."

chapter 23

CRIME SCENE - DO NOT CROSS CRIME SCENE - DO NOT CROSS

DETECTIVE FORD

I've broken every traffic law on my way home. A ride that normally takes over forty minutes, today I've done in half, counting down every second in between.

Perez and Baez are behind me in an unmarked SUV and blaring their siren. Most people make way for us, a few looking at my car as though I'm a fleeing criminal, and had this been any other day, I would've found it amusing.

Not today. Not when the love of my life is alone and scared.

When she could be—

No. I won't let my thoughts travel to the worst-case scenario. She has to be okay.

There is no other option.

Life couldn't be so cruel as to gift me Ava and then take her away.

Grabbing my phone, I send Perez a text, telling him to cut the siren off. We're a street from my building, and the last thing we want is to alert Jason of our presence. All I have on my side is the act of surprise, and I plan to use it.

There's a bullet with his name on it, and I want it lodged deep within his brain before he touches a hair on Ava's head.

"Lord, please don't let him hurt her. Let me get there in time," I say, throwing my car into park in front of my building. My eyes flick to the left and notice that Stein and McGrady's car is still there, but with no sign of them inside.

I pull out my gun and signal with my arm toward the car for Perez to follow up. My gut tells me there's more than one rat in the building—a confirmation made a second later when Meyers himself walks around the corner with another man I've never seen before.

They're laughing, wiping their hands on a hand towel, but not before I catch sight of the blood. "Those two dumb fucks were easy enough."

"Predictably boring," Meyers says, chuckling as he looks toward his companion. "They were pigs in a slaughterhouse."

The man nods and shoots him a smirk. "And how long before we can bounce?"

"Soon." Meyers looks down at his hand, picking something out from underneath his nail bed. "Once the cunt...the fuck!" He doesn't get to finish, eyes snapping up and going wide as his friend falls. Blood spreads rapidly, seeping from his chest and staining the concrete floor beneath him. His eyes go from the dead man to mine, and his entire body goes rigid, fear coloring his features. "F-Ford. Captain. What are you doing here?"

"I'm here to finish this." That's all I say while placing my gun back in the holster. Then, before he can utter another word, I tackle his pathetic ass to the floor, landing a straight punch to his face. Then another. The bone crunches beneath my fingers, blood splattering against my skin. I revel in it. In his screams of pain. In his pathetic attempt to push me off.

"Please."

"Fuck you," I spit out, elbow coming down right across his cheek. A gash follows, large and stretching across his red skin. It's not enough. Nothing but death will ever be.

"Enough," I hear Baez yell, and I'm half tempted to laugh. I'm gone. Nothing but his death will satisfy my need for revenge. To pay him back for every life taken.

He might not have killed them, but he helped. Blood is on his hands.

Two hands grab me, and I pull free, landing another blow to his already bruised face. And again. I don't stop, and this time, no one stops me until I'm satisfied. His head hits the concrete, bouncing a few times before I pull back. I'm silent as I stand, not looking at anyone—or at the few cruisers that have arrived since we got here—and walk to the entrance of the building.

People call my name.

Someone tries to pull me back.

I'd kill them all if it came to it.

The silence follows me up the stairs, every flight up taking me to another plane of anger. I've never experienced this level of ire. Every floor up fills my body with a pulsing energy. My muscles coil, limbs shaking.

My floor is desolate when I reach it. Nothing.

No signs of anyone.

My door is closed, and just as I place my key inside the lock, the blast of a gun breaks the silence. It's loud, and so is the pure scream of panic that comes from Ava's body.

Fuck the structure. I kick it in and rush toward the sound of her voice. They're inside my room. The closer I get, the clearer I can hear his words and how he taunts her.

"Come out, little one," he croons just as I step within sight. He's sitting on my bed, twirling his gun while watching the closet door.

He doesn't see me. He's too sure of himself. "The faster I correct this defiant behavior, the happier you'll be. A little pain for a lifetime of my love and devotion."

"Please stop," I hear Ava cry out, the fear in her voice palpable. "Leave, and I won't call the cops."

"Not until I break you, love. Until you bleed for me." Lyle looks a mess, dirty and desperate. His arm shakes as he points the gun toward the door, finger on the trigger. "We can do this the easy way or hard way, Sugar. Your choice."

"Leave!" That scream is pure horror and pain. It strikes across my chest as if it were a cat-o'-nine-tails whip with sharp metal tips. A punishment for not being here to protect her.

"Open the door, Ava, and I'll begin to forgive you."

"I'm not yours!"

"Wrong choice."

Jason still hasn't noticed me. Something about the way he's acting makes me think that he's under the influence of a narcotic: eyes glassy and body slightly trembling. And it's while his hand shakes and another bullet dislodges from the gun that I fully enter the room. Ava screams from the other side, and the phone inside my pocket vibrates within seconds of my entry.

Behind me, I can hear the rest of our team pausing. They're waiting on my call, but my focus is on him. My target. The next body to fall.

As that finger twitches again, ready to fire, I pull my own. Watching in almost slow motion as a bullet leaves my gun and flies through the air at a speed he can't detect. It hits his side, right between his ribs, and he falls back onto my mattress.

His shirt—old and dirty—is colored red. The splotch grows as the seconds tick by.

His eyes shift to mine, surprised but not shocked to see me. Instead, a cruel smirk forms on his lips. "About time you showed up, Detective. Nice to see you again."

"Rot in hell, Porter." I'm not playing his game. Instead, I pull the trigger again. And again. The second and third bullets hit his midsection, his body convulsing on the bed, and yet, Lyle still fires his weapon. It hits the drywall encasing the steel structure, and I reciprocate with the same amount of anger.

I empty the first clip as my girl yells from inside. The second is merely for my amusement,

bullet after bullet entering his body, and the fucker still rises from the bed. He comes toward me, bloody and knocking on death's door but unwilling to give up.

He stumbles, pointing his gun, but when he tries to fire back...nothing. He's out of bullets and losing blood fast. One step forward becomes a crashing fall to the floor, and still, I do not pity a dying man.

Fuck him.

This pain is nothing compared to what the asshole deserves.

Pulling my other guns from its holster, I stand over his semi-lifeless body. Our eyes meet. His next breath is almost choking, and still, I fire once more. Right between the eyes.

The small hole in his forehead is proof of his passing. One stuttered breath, and he's gone.

No longer a danger to my girl.

Without pausing, I drop my weapon and rush toward the closet, banging on the door. "Baby, it's me. Open, please."

"Eli?"

"I'm here, sweetheart." It takes a minute or two for her to open, but when she does, the relief in her eyes almost bowls me over. Ava flies into my arms, wrapping her small body around mine and clinging—holding me tight with her eyes closed as I turn her away from his lifeless form.

She's shaking. Afraid. Sobbing. "He...I..."

"Are you hurt?" I want to pull back and check her out, but the way she's clinging to me makes it impossible. And I wouldn't take my comfort from her. I'm here to be whatever she needs. "Can you answer one thing, beautiful? Did he—?"

"He didn't, but I kicked him. I fought back..." a sob catches in her throat "...oh, God!"

"I've got you," I whisper against her forehead, my arms wrapping tight and giving her the comfort she needs. "He's dead. No more fear."

"Are you sure?" A tremor rocks her small body.

"I swear." With two fingers, I tip her face up and out of its hiding spot in my neck. Watery blue eyes meet mine, and in them, I see my forever. Home. It's a moment that tethers me to this earth solely so I can walk by her side. Those three words sit on the tip of my tongue, and although I've said them before, right this second they take on a more profound meaning.

Losing her would've killed me. Taken my very soul as I followed her into the next life. This courageous woman in my arms is my life. Everything. "Ava," I choke up, hands trembling as I pull her impossibly closer. Lift her and press her chest against my racing heart. "I love you. All of you. There is no one else for me in this life and every single one that follows."

"I love you, too. Christ, when he said that you—"

"We're here, and that's all that matters. For the rest of our lives, it'll be just you and me."

"Against the world."

"Something either of you want to explain?" Perez comes up behind me then, but I pay him no mind. While I hid this—our relationship—he hid his own. Not that I care, but I won't let him be a hypocrite, either.

"Not really." I shrug, not taking my eyes off my girl.

"Baby, I—"

"Ford, you—"

They both start, but I hold a hand up to silence the two. Walking out of the room and away from the last reminder of her nightmare, I take us into the living room and sit down with her in my lap. Perez follows, eyeing me, but takes a seat across from us.

Watching. Gauging.

"You know." That's all he says.

"I do." Ava stiffens but doesn't leap up. To ease her tension, I begin rubbing her back in slow, soothing strokes. It takes a minute or two, but she does calm down and then melts into me, burrowing against my chest as the stress of the day catches up.

People come in and out of the apartment—cops and a medical team, all checking and documenting to corroborate my story and, later, hers, with the physical evidence. No one speaks to us outside of that. They let us be for the time being, and I keep my eyes on Perez the entire time. Even raise a brow to help him get on with the explanation that, to be honest, isn't needed, but I know he'll give.

"How?"

"Looking into possible connections to the case, familial or friends."

"Why not say anything?" he asks, scratching his chin, not the least bit sorry.

"Because I get it." At that, Ava looks up at me, remorse in her puffy eyes, but I shake my head, letting her know I'm not the least bit angry. "She's your niece, Cap. You were just trying to protect Miss Perez here—not to be confused with a Perry. Good choice on the last name change, though. It's close enough that she wouldn't mess up. However, I did pick up on a slight change in her accent when upset—more Spaniard. That's something you do, too."

"So, you're not upset?" Ava asks, her tone hopeful.

"Not in the least." Lowering my face to hers, I kiss her lips once. A soft peck. "All that matters is that I have you, and you're safe. Everything else is inconsequential."

"I do love you, Elijah."

"With all my heart."

"Looks like I'll be giving you the talk her parents won't be able to," he says, and my eyes leave her sweet face and shift toward his. "It's my duty, after all."

"More like you'll get a kick out of it, *Tio*." Ava shakes her head, still wiping at the stray tears falling. This ordeal will leave a mark on her. On us. There's no getting over a traumatic event like this one, but I'll spend the rest of my life watching over and slaying her demons.

"So true." He lets out a low chuckle but sobers just as quickly. "Besides, I trust Ford. I knew he would keep you safe."

"Is that your way of saying you approve?" Perez nods at my question. "Good. Because I'm not going anywhere."

"What about when she goes back to Dallas?"

That makes me pause. It's not something either of us have discussed or thought about. To be honest, we haven't had the time to, but without a second of hesitation, I know the answer. "Where she goes—"

"My home is with him. Here or there. It makes no difference to me." Her words pierce me straight in the heart. So much conviction. So much trust in me.

It also helps to settle some of my nerves.

She wants this. Even after everything that animal put her through, my girl puts her faith in us.

Til death do us part. And even that won't be enough.

Ava is my everything. The piece of my soul I didn't know was missing.

She was born to be mine.

epilogue #1

CRIME SCENE - DO NOT CROSS CRIME SCENE - DO NOT CROSS

DETECTIVE FORD

Six Months Later...

"Oh, God," Ava moans, body arching as she rides me. Her hips are picking up speed with each gyration, while a beautiful flush sweeps across her chest. She's simply breathtaking every day, but when lost in her pleasure, my little baker is ethereal. A motherfucking goddess. "So good. So close, baby."

Her thighs shake on either side of me, tightening against my hips while those blue eyes remain on mine. They're heavy-lidded and full of so much love that my chest aches. That my cock throbs against her walls, and my hands clutch her hips, fingers digging in deep.

Her want mirrors my own.

Her hunger is felt down to my bones, and I crave it. That spark. That pulse that flows from our bodies, cocooning us in a battle of love and lust and happiness that I never thought I'd be a part of.

She's mine, and I am hers. End of.

"*Fuck*, Ava. That's it. Squeeze me just like that," I hiss between clenched teeth, one hand guiding her movements while the other lands a sharp spank. Then another. I alternate each strike in intensity—reveling in the heat coming from her soft skin as each slap blooms and spreads. Moreover, my girl likes it. Loves the bite of pain as my cock grazes her cervix with each upward thrust.

Her hips move faster.

My strokes are harder.

The sound of skin meeting skin is obscene in its beauty, just like her little whimpers. "I'm so close, Papi. God, you own me."

"I feel you, my pretty love." I smack her right cheek a final time and then grind her against me, keeping a tight hold—not letting her move—so I can fuck her with brutal pumps of my hips. She lets out a cry, shaking, but I don't stop. "You feel so good, Ava. I can feel you clench with each stroke—tighten around my cock to keep me buried deep. Is that what you want?"

"Never want this to end." It's a breathy whisper. A low, keening sound that settles on the tip of my cock and causes my balls to tighten. I want her full of my come. Soaked in my essence and, hopefully soon, giving me a child.

She'll be carrying my name. Attached to me for life.

Becoming the mother of my child.

The only woman I swear to love for the rest of this life and any that follow.

"Always." Slipping a hand between us, I place my thumb over her clit and put just enough pressure that she shakes and throws her head back, a desperate cry slipping past her lips. It's her tell. That sound gives her away; it's a delicious warning I revel in each time we're together. "Look at me."

At my demand, those beautiful orbs focus on mine, and I see everything I will ever need in them. There's not a single ounce of doubt in my body that this woman was made for me. A true gift.

My other hand leaves her hip and grasps the back of her neck, pulling her down to me, chest to chest now, as my hips never stop pumping into her. She tightens and tries to match my thrust, to chase the bite of heaven within her reach, but I'm relentless as I circle my finger over that tiny bundle of nerves.

We share a breath.

Lips hovering.

Eyes on each other.

"I love you." Ava's tone is just above a whisper before she kisses me, slow and sweet, with every ounce of the love I'm drowning in. "You make me so happy, Elijah. You've given me everything."

"You're wrong. Not everything." Adding a bit more pressure, I circle her clit twice and hold still. Her walls pulse, she shivers, and I raise her off my dick until just the tip sits at her opening.

A tease. A wicked promise of what I'm going to do.

"What're you...fuck!" Without a word, I slam her down, giving my girl that last bit of pleasurable pain she needs to fall over the edge. My hips are relentless, fucking up into her with a steady and hard stroke.

"Please." One word. Desperation. Her need.

A light sheen of sweat gleams across her forehead, and her brows pucker. Those lips I love part, and she exhales; her warm breath is a caress across my mouth, and I take hers once more in a hard kiss.

Each swipe of my tongue over her bottom lip is an *I love you.* Each groan that leaves my chest is an oath to always protect and cherish.

"Come for me, Ava."

"I'm...shit!" she whimpers as my fingers tighten their hold on her neck, not letting her move an inch. She's in my control. Taking what I gift her.

"Now, baby. Give me what's always been mine." No sooner has

the last words slipped past my lips that she tightens—chokes on a silent scream. Her orgasm rocks me, a vice-like grip so hard and warm that my release quickly follows. It's hard and messy, and I don't stop thrusting as she milks every last drop from my cock.

Not even after she lies on my chest, completely spent and satiated, do I pause. Not until I feel the last tremor pass through her tired limbs and her pussy eases its hold.

Then, I close my eyes as we just lie there in her small bed back in Dallas, surrounded by boxes and memories of her old life—a life she's transferring to Los Angeles to build a new one with me. No more rentals while my apartment was sold. No more never-ending searches for the perfect place to start this new stage of our lives. Now, we get it all. I will give her that fairy-tale life she deserves and then some.

There's no denying that the road here has been difficult, full of complications and tears.

And while I wish we would've met under different circumstances; we both agree that it's the ending that matters.

After Lyle's death, Ava dealt with a hurricane of emotions and guilt—regret and total despair—but through it all, she never pushed me away. I was her constant.

She chose me. Always.

And I was there for her through each therapy session and then the tears. Through all the hurt and the years of anger, she let go of. It was hard. Still brutal at points, but it has brought us closer together. We've both had to deal with the aftermath and have come out stronger because we have each other.

For better or worse. In sickness and health.

I don't know how long we lay there with her body on my chest before I feel her stare. And fuck me, it's hard to hold in my smile when I hear her impatient huff.

Cracking open one eye, I watch her watching me. "Something on your mind?"

"You could say that."

"Speak up or forever hold your peace." Yeah, I'm baiting her.

Ava's eyes leave mine for a split second to look down at her left hand. "Funny you should use those words."

"Funny that you're making me wait for that three-letter word."

"Is there a question I'm missing?"

"No."

"No?" She cocks her brow and purses those succulent lips, yet I see the hint of a smile there.

"Yes." My mouth quirks up into a cheesy grin, and she rolls her eyes. "You know I'm right."

"So cocky."

"Exactly."

Ava's eyes fill with unshed tears, and her lips tremble while stretching wide into a smile. "Then, in that case, who am I to argue? Yes."

"There was never a doubt, baby." Rolling us over, I thrust deeper, causing her to let out a low moan. I'm hard again, always for her. "I'm going to spend the rest of my life worshipping you. Loving you. Making sure that you never doubt just how important you are to me." Lifting the hand wearing my ring, I kiss it while never taking my eyes off hers. "Thank you for trusting me with your heart, Ava. It's a treasure I'll always keep safe and protected. I love you, sweetheart. Always will."

"I love you, too. So much," she says, voice thick with emotion before arching up to kiss my lips. This kiss is different than all the ones before; it's the start of a new beginning. Of our family, and as I pump my hips slowly, another warm thought comes to mind.

I'm not waiting another second to start this next stage of *us*.

Not when I can fly us to Vegas tonight and make her fully mine.

Not when I can fall asleep tonight with her as my wife.

"How do you feel about getting—"

"Yes," she moans out, eyes rolling back when I tilt my hips, changing the angle of my thrust. "I don't want to wait either."

"Tonight." That's all I say before getting lost in my fiancée's touch. In her scent. Her love.

Because the next time I take her, she will bear my name.

She will be my wife.

epilogue #2

AVA

Two Years Later...

I'm nervous.

Excited.

Scared out of my mind in the best possible way. The room around me is abuzz with people talking and eating, enjoying the fruits of my labor, and still, I can't focus on the task at hand.

I've been standing at this counter for twenty minutes now, watching the door and waiting. Sure, I give an occasional smile or make small talk with those perusing the display case, but I'm on autopilot, just repeating what flavors are new, the weather, and the latest trends in tourism.

Tourism—something that when you live near water changes with each season. You go from snowbirds to internationals to convention season in the blink of an eye. We get them all, and I've come to love each one.

It's made my eight months in business a challenge, yet fun. My menu changes with the seasons, too, and I'm known for the eclectic yet posh little tastes of heaven my shelves sell out of each day.

"I need three servings of *you* with extra sugar," a voice I'm all too familiar with whispers against my neck before placing a kiss there. His strong arms encircle my waist and pick me up, turning me toward his handsome face. "Hi."

My smile matches his. Cheesy and goofy. "Hello, handsome. Long day?" And like every day Elijah comes in, I find myself lost in those beautiful eyes and the way his broad shoulders feel beneath my fingertips as I smooth his dress shirt.

He's my hot detective. Mine.

And now I'm going to gladly share him with someone else for the rest of our lives. Someone that will grow and learn and know that they're loved unconditionally by us.

"Any time away from you is hard." He punctuates this by subtly pressing his hard length against my stomach. No one pays us any mind, especially not my staff or the regulars who know I completely belong to this wonderful man. "How are you feeling today? Have you eaten?"

"She hasn't had lunch yet," Margot, one of my baristas, calls over her shoulder as she walks toward the coffee machine.

"Is that right?" There's mirth in his eyes mixed with a hint of reproach.

"Waiting on you," I say, looking up at him from beneath my long lashes.

"Hmmm." He gives a mock sigh, and then I'm airborne, being carried toward my office. "Let's get you fed."

"Aren't we heading in the wrong direction for that?" Looking behind us, I lock eyes with his mother and smile. Outside of Elijah, she's been my rock in the aftermath of Lyle and his obsession. Has become a second mother to me and a confidant—understands without judgment.

She held my hand during the trial and sentencing of my ex-best friend and their accomplice. They got a life sentence, and to me, that still isn't enough. Not after how many lives were destroyed due to their sickness.

She hugged me as I fell apart due to the stress and then celebrated when it was all over.

It's because of her that I was able to process internally what happened. She's the reason I wrote that tragedy out in the form of a book that I'll never publish, but the process was cathartic. I was able to get my emotions and thoughts down on paper. Admit and deal with the survivor's guilt that still lingers, but I know and accept now that the blame isn't on me.

I'm a victim. I'm a survivor. I'm alive.

Nodding, she does an excited jump/shake while giving me two thumbs up.

"We'll order something and get it delivered," Eli grumbles, a little bit of impatience coloring his tone. "Need my woman alone for a bit."

It's hard not to roll my eyes or smile at his mom when he says that, but I do, and it's a good thing because, within seconds, we're inside my office with the door closed. The last thing I want to do is ruin this surprise. I want him completely caught off guard.

Elijah walks around my desk and sits down with me in his lap. He also doesn't say anything about the two plates with dome lids atop them. Or the fact that the one closest to us has a balloon attached.

I knew we'd end up here at some point. Had a bet going with his mom about it, too.

She thought he'd sneak me away for a romantic lunch.

And I said he'd want the privacy of my office with a solid steel door, the latter of which he insisted on.

"Well," I hedge, looking at him with a mock impatient look. "Aren't you going to feed me?"

"Food first, or my cock?"

"So scandalous." I laugh, slapping his chest while seriously considering the latter. Having some fun first wouldn't be a bad idea. "But—"

"I will after." Elijah winks at me and then proceeds to lift the ballooned dome. "Something you want to tell me, Wife?"

There's a small cake inside. It's his favorite: a triple-layer dessert all in chocolate. There's no fancy decorating or anything that would give away the purpose unless you open the small note sitting in front of it.

Something he does without prompting. He tears it open, and when he reads the line written in my chicken scratch, happy eyes meet mine.

Happy Baby Day!

"Are you saying...are we?"

"You're going to be a daddy," I whisper, the tears I've been fighting spilling down my cheeks as his own get watery. This is something we've wanted. Talked about.

And to finally have this blessing... No words.

"I love you so much, Ava." Strong hands cup my face and pull me toward a hungry mouth. His kiss is full of love and devotion. Of need and our shared happiness. "Thank you for giving me your heart. For starting a family with me." Another peck, this one lingers and nibbles before he pulls back. "You've made me the luckiest son of a bitch to walk this earth."

"I'm so thankful for you. For us." My bottom lip trembles as I take one of his hands in mine, pulling it down to my still-flat stomach. "You and this baby are my everything."

"And you're *mine*," he says, the emphasis and possessiveness aren't lost on me, but before I can give him a snarky rebuttal, Elijah's kissing me again. Loving me. Showing me with tender touches and whispered words just how much I mean to him.

Filling every inch of my soul with his beautiful essence.

His mark.

He always says he's keeping me for life, but the truth is…

I'm the one never letting go.

Not of him or the beautiful little girl we had seven months later. Chloe Heather Ford came into the world kicking her tiny legs and screaming. She wrapped her father around her little fingers and filled my heart with so much joy while those closest to us celebrated the newest member of our family.

We built something incredible. Loved hard and beyond all comprehension.

And as my husband lovingly spoke to our daughter hours after her birth; I vowed to help her navigate his *fatherly* craziness. "You, sweet angel, will never be allowed to date. Not ever. Daddy has a lot of guns to make this happen, too."

Over protective. Always present.

My hero.

God, I love him.

The End.

COMING THIS SUMMER…

One kiss will doom him.
One bite will claim her.

For more info on SIREN'S KISS and FERAL BEASTS, please sign

up for my newsletter and ADD this to your TBR on Goodreads. I will be sharing a pre-order and all the smutty/goodies very soon.

Goodreads: https://www.goodreads.com/book/show/230233285-siren-s-kiss-and-feral-beasts

Newsletter Sign-Up On My Website: elenamreyes.com

This will have the following:
Enemies To Lovers
Fated Mates
Revenge
Pirates
Sirens
Knots
Shifters
Tropical Island Smut
Squirting
Spanking
Size Difference/Bulging
Wants Her Bred
And So Much More…

The Beautiful Sinner Series are all interconnected standalones full of suspense and romance and an OTT alpha willing to burn the world to the ground for the woman he loves! It's sexy and has an edge of darkness that will leave you breathless! #MAFIAROMANCE

Now Live!

SIN (#1)
COVET (#2)
MINE (#3)
YOURS (#4)
RISQUE #5
OWN #6

BEAUTIFUL SINNER SPIN-OFFS

BEAUTIFUL SINNER SERIES

CORRUPT
SAVAGE KISS
ONE RULE
MY SINFUL VALENTINE

DARK PARANORMAL ROMANCE

SERIES ORDER:

LITTLE LIES
LITTLE MATE
HALF TRUTHS: THEN
HALF TRUTHS: NOW
OMISSION: PART ONE
OMISSION: PART TWO

<u>FATE'S BITE SPIN-OFFS:</u>

COME TO ME (2026)
THE HUNT (OCT 2025)

ABOUT THE AUTHOR

Elena M. Reyes was born and raised in Miami, Florida. She is the epitome of a Floridian and if she could live in her beloved flip-flops, she would.

As a small child, she was always intrigued with all forms of art—whether it was dancing to island rhythms, or painting with any medium she could get her hands on. Her first taste of writing came to her during her fifth-grade year when her class was prompted to participate in the D. A. R. E. Program and write an essay on what they'd learned.

Her passion for reading over the years has amassed her with hours of pleasure. It wasn't until she stumbled upon fanfiction that her thirst to write overtook her world. She now resides in Central Florida with her husband and son, spending all her down time letting her creativity flow and characters grow.

Newsletter Sign-Up & Website:
https://www.elenamreyes.com/

Find My Books Here:
https://www.bookbub.com/authors/elena-m-reyes

Email: Reyes139ff@gmail.com

facebook.com/ElenaMReyesAuthor
instagram.com/elenar139
tiktok.com/@authorelenamreyes
bookbub.com/profile/elena-m-reyes
bsky.app/profile/elenamreyes.bsky.social
amazon.com/stores/Elena-M.-Reyes/author

ALSO BY:

<u>FATE'S BITE SERIES:</u>

LITTLE LIES
LITTLE MATE
HALF TRUTHS: THEN
HALF TRUTHS: NOW
OMISSION: PART ONE
OMISSION: PART TWO

<u>FATE'S BITE SPIN-OFFS:</u>

COME TO ME (2026)
THE HUNT (OCT 2025)

<u>BEAUTIFUL SINNER SERIES</u>

Each book is a standalone.

SIN (#1)
COVET (#2)
MINE (#3)
YOURS (#4)
RISQUE #5
OWN #6

BEAUTIFUL SINNER SPIN-OFFS

CORRUPT
SAVAGE KISS
ONE RULE
MY SINFUL VALENTINE

MARKED SERIES

Marking Her #1
Marking Him #2
Scars #2.5
Marked #3

I SAW YOU SERIES

I Saw You
I Love You #1.5

TEASING HANDS DUET

Teasing Hands #1
Taunting Lips #2

SAFE ROMANCE:

Taste Of You
Doctor's Orders
Back To You

STANDALONES:

Craving Sugar
Stolen Kisses
Cupid's Naughty Elf

www.ingramcontent.com/pod-product-compliance
Lightning Source LLC
Chambersburg PA
CBHW020408210626
46816CB00006BB/2180

9781957375304